Dear Reader,

There's something about the tropics that automatically turns up the heat on a classic love story, whether it's the possibilities offered by miles of uninhabited beaches, the magnificence and peril of the surrounding ocean, or the way the sun seems to glisten off the rips and folds of salty, bronzed skin. I hoped to capture some of that sultriness when I wrote *Return to Santa Flores,* which is set in a small resort town in the Bahamas where the air is dripping with passion and temptation, and there's a little bit of taboo running just beneath the surface. Add to that a romance that is so fiery it drives the characters nearly out of their minds with shared jealousy, frustration, and obsession, but is so enticing that they can't help but cross over the threshold into forbidden territory.

Steve Jason is the type of character I love to write—sexy, self-absorbed, and in control; a playboy who's seemingly disinterested in any one woman, but could have a dozen lined up in a minute if he so much as snapped his fingers. But it's

Jenny Cashman who catches his attention with her quiet sophistication and plucky resolve. Over the years, as he watches Jenny evolve into a strong and beautiful woman, his duty becomes to not only protect her from the evils of the outside world, but to resist the desire to possess her as his own treasure. As many of you know, I tend to cast headstrong and self-assured female characters, so I had a lot of fun helping Jenny discover her sexuality and independence, as she matures from the child who once idly built sandcastles by the shore to a woman who knows her own mind and heart.

Return to Santa Flores is a story that I felt completely transported by while writing, and I hope you are as excited as I am to "return" to Steve and Jenny's exotic and lustrous world.

Iris Johansen

PRAISE FOR IRIS JOHANSEN

"Iris Johansen knows how to win instant fans."
—Associated Press

"Iris Johansen is a powerful writer."
—*The Atlanta Journal-Constitution*

"[Iris Johansen is] one of the romance genre's
finest treasures."
—*Romantic Times*

"A master among storytellers."
—*Affaire de Coeur*

"Johansen serves up a diverting romance
and plot twists worthy of a mystery novel."
—*Publishers Weekly*

"[Iris] Johansen has . . . a magical quality."
—*Library Journal*

"[Johansen is] a consummate artist who wields her pen with
extraordinary power and grace."
—*Rave Reviews*

"Iris Johansen is a bestselling author for the best
reason—she's a wonderful storyteller."
—CATHERINE COULTER

"Iris Johansen is incomparable."
—TAMI HOAG

ALSO BY IRIS JOHANSEN

IRIS JOHANSEN

~

Return to Santa Flores

BANTAM BOOKS
NEW YORK

2013 Bantam Books Mass Market Edition

Copyright © 1984 by Iris Johansen

Published in the United States by Bantam Books, an imprint of The Random House Publishing Group, a division of Random House, Inc., New York.

BANTAM BOOKS and the HOUSE colophon are registered trademarks of Random House, Inc.

Originally published in paperback in the United States by Bantam Loveswept, an imprint of The Random House Publishing Group, a division of Random House, Inc., in 1984.

ISBN 978-0-345-53954-0
eBook ISBN 978-0-345-53955-7

Cover design: Eileen Carey
Cover image: © Julia Savchenko

Printed in the United States of America

www.bantamdell.com

9 8 7 6 5 4 3 2 1

Bantam Books mass market edition: August 2013

Return to
Santa Flores

ONE

HE WAS THE most beautiful human being she had ever seen.

The first tentative rays of the sun bathed the white sand with a radiant glow and cast a patina of gold over the figure of the man. He appeared to reflect not only the glow of the sun but a boundless vitality.

Apollo, she thought again in breathless admiration, as she had the first time she had seen him four days ago. It had been sunrise then, too, as he strode along the beach like a god from Olympus, not noticing her sitting with her back pressed against the stone sea wall. His eyes were a brilliant sapphire blue in a face of lean classical perfection. His hair was dark gold and seemed to radiate the morning light. He was dressed in dark bathing trunks, and his tall muscular body had a virile toughness that was as striking as the handsomeness of his face.

She'd never spoken to him, content to sit and watch each day as he walked briskly down the beach from the hotel, throwing his towel on the sand and entering the water with a pagan enjoyment that was more sea god than sun god. But she knew that she must speak today.

"Don't go into the water."

The man whirled, startled, his eyes wary, his face suddenly taut and dangerous. The tough menace of his stance frightened her for a moment, but as he observed the small figure sitting cross-legged in the sand, he relaxed and raised an eyebrow quizzically.

"Were you speaking to me?" He gazed curiously at the little girl. She couldn't have been more than nine, he thought. She was a fragile-looking child, her thin face dominated by enormous gray eyes framed with sweeping black lashes. Her long, straight dark hair was pushed carelessly away from her face and hung in a shiny curtain to her waist.

The eyes were almost silver, he noticed absently, as she continued to gaze at him with quaint solemnity.

She nodded, and lowered her eyes to the sand castle she was building so painstakingly, cutting a window in a turret with one careful finger. "Don't go into the sea today," she repeated, not looking at him. "Portuguese man-of-war were sighted yesterday afternoon just off the coast. Esmeralda told me that they can be dangerous."

"Indeed they can," he said wryly. Since he'd extended his operations to this small island in the Bahamas, he had heard much of this deadly sea life, whose poison attacked the nervous system causing severe illness and in a few cases even death. "And who, pray, is the knowledgeable Esmeralda?"

"Esmeralda Haskins. She's a maid at the hotel." The child explained matter of factly, gesturing to the large gleaming white building at the far end of the beach. "She's engaged to Joe St. Clair. He's a fisherman."

"And I presume it was Joe, the fisherman, who told Esmeralda, the maid, about the man-of-war," he surmised, his lips quirking.

"That's right." She added another window to the castle.

He wondered why he was standing here, trying to converse with this taciturn elf. He was not a man who had any time for children, but there was a grave maturity about this one that was intriguing. He speculated on which one of his hotel staff had fathered the child. It was unlikely that she was the child of a guest. The faded blue shorts and shirt she wore were definitely shabby. It wasn't plausible that anyone who could afford the luxury rates at the Santa Flores Hotel and Casino would dress their offspring so poorly.

"Aren't you a little young to be out here alone at this hour?" he asked.

She looked up. "I'm eleven," she told him seriously. "I look younger because I'm small for my age."

"Won't someone be worrying about you?" he persisted.

The long, dark lashes masked her eyes as she looked down again, her hands busy in the sand. "No."

He shrugged and picked up his towel, making a

mental note to find out who was so negligent as to permit a child of eleven to wander unsupervised on a deserted beach at dawn.

As he turned to go back to the hotel, the child spoke again. "You work at the hotel, don't you?" The silver eyes were gravely enquiring, the small hands clasped serenely on her crossed knees.

"In a manner of speaking," he said coolly. "But why do you assume that? I could be a guest."

She shrugged. "It's too early for hotel guests. In a place like this they stay up as long as the casino's open, and then they don't get out of bed until noon the next day."

"You're very well informed," he said mockingly. Then he caught himself, amazed that he was talking to this child as if she were a contemporary.

She was gazing at him thoughtfully, noting the mockery and accepting it with composure. But he had the odd sensation that she was withdrawing within herself, much like a night blooming cereus that folds up its petals when exposed to the powerful light of the sun.

It was suddenly intolerable that he might have hurt this strange waif. He smiled with a heart catching warmth that would have astounded the few who claimed they knew him. "I didn't thank you for telling me about the man-of-war," he said. "You might have saved my life."

She shook her head, but said nothing.

"My name is Steve Jason," he added coaxingly. "Don't you think it's about time we introduced ourselves?"

"I'm Jenny," she said hesitantly. "Jennifer Antonia Cashman."

"I'm very happy to meet you, Jennifer Antonia Cashman."

She studied him for a moment as if wondering if she could put her trust in him, then she smiled. He caught his breath involuntarily. It was an incredibly lovely smile, lighting up the somberness of her thin, gypsy face with a special fascination. "And I'm very happy to meet you, Steve Jason," she answered with old-fashioned formality.

He lingered, oddly reluctant to leave her here on her own. "Why don't you walk back to the hotel with me?" he asked. "Your parents will expect you for breakfast, surely."

She shook her head, surveying her sand castle again. "I'll stay here a little while, thank you."

"Well at least tell me your parents' names and what they do, so I can tell them where to find you," he said in exasperation.

"That won't be necessary."

"Answer me, Jenny," he ordered.

He thought for a moment that she was going to defy him. Then she looked up at him, her silver eyes steady. "My father is Henry Cashman. He's a gambler."

A puzzled frown wrinkled his forehead. "Do you mean he's a dealer at the casino?"

Jenny shook her head. "No, he doesn't work at the hotel," she said softly. "He just gambles."

Suddenly the child was on her feet and was flying down the beach toward the hotel, her dark hair floating behind her like a glossy banner.

Steve Jason gazed after her quicksilver figure, startled momentarily by the abruptness of her departure. Then, his sapphire eyes thoughtful, he slung his towel around his neck and started to walk slowly back to the hotel.

"Why are you staring at me like that, funny face?" Steve asked idly, letting the white sand pour slowly from his cupped hand. "Do I have a smudge on my face?" He was sitting beside little Jenny, his face lifted to enjoy the caress of the early morning sun. He had been conscious for some time of the surreptitious glances she had been giving him. He had grown used to the tranquility of the child and no longer thought it unusual. This sign of self consciousness in her aroused his curiosity.

"I was thinking that you reminded me of someone," she confessed awkwardly.

He raised his eyebrow inquiringly.

"Apollo," she said with a rush, her thin face suddenly pink.

He exploded with laughter and her face turned even redder. He controlled his amusement with an effort, knowing the fragile dignity of the child. A strange friendship had grown between them in the past week. Every morning she was there by the sea wall, and he had become accustomed to joining her after his swim and watching the sunrise before he returned to the hotel.

Jenny was a completely restful companion. She

rarely spoke, and when she did, her conversation was never banal. She listened with such receptive interest that he found himself rambling on about subjects completely outside her experience. She had an almost crystal transparency, and was the most totally honest person he had ever known. If she didn't wish to answer a question, she would simply remain silent. If she did speak, the answer would be completely truthful, even if it caused her discomfort as this one obviously did.

"You do look like Apollo," she insisted. "I noticed it the first time I saw you."

He was not embarrassed by the comparison. He knew without vanity that he was good looking. It was a fact that he used with the same cool calculation as he did every other asset he possessed.

"He's an old buddy of yours?" he teased.

She looked up at him scornfully. It was unusual for him to talk down to her. "I saw his picture in a book," she said sternly. "It was a statue in a place called the Vatican."

"Isn't that a little heavy reading for an eleven year old?"

"It wasn't a real book," she explained. "It was in one of the guide books I collected in Rome."

It was the first time Jenny had volunteered any information about her background. She seemed to live totally in the present. He asked with careful carelessness, "You've been to the Vatican?"

She shook her head. "No, I just read the guide book. I collect them, you know. They have such beautiful pictures. I have a lovely one from Athens on the Parthenon. Ariadne used to give me all the ones she found when she cleaned the rooms and emptied the waste baskets. The tourists always tossed them away when they came back from their tours."

"Ariadne was a maid in the hotel in Athens?" he guessed.

She nodded. "Ariadne Aristophas. Isn't that a lovely name? She was awfully pretty. She was only working until she got enough money for her dowry. She was engaged to Demetrius Popolus, and it would have been a great disgrace if she had come to him empty handed," she finished solemnly.

"I can understand that," he said with equal gravity, enjoying her rare talkativeness. "What other guide books have you collected?"

She reeled off a list of European cities that was startling. He whistled. "You're quite a well-traveled lady, Jenny."

"Yes, I know," she said absently, her thoughts still on her guide books. "I think I like the ones from London best. But I wonder why the British like red so much. Did you know that even their telephone booths are red?"

"I wasn't aware of that. Did you see the Tower of London?"

"No," she answered wistfully, then brightened. "But we passed Trafalgar Square on the way to the airport."

He smothered an impatient curse, conscious of a growing dislike of Jenny's neglectful parent. Curiosity had goaded him to make a few discreet inquiries regarding Henry Cashman, and what he had learned was not encouraging. The man appeared to be one of the breed of itinerant professional gamblers who wandered over the face of the globe, gleaning a precarious livelihood from gambling casinos and high stakes games on cruise ships.

Though the man himself was a picture of sartorial elegance, Jason had never seen Jenny in anything but the shabbiest of playclothes. She obviously had been dragged helter-skelter across half of Europe, and had not even been taken to the most commonplace tourist attractions. She seemed to have no friends. His eyes ran over her small form critically. She was thin as a rail. Did the bastard even see that she had enough to eat?

Why did the thought upset him so much, he asked himself impatiently. He had always been a loner. He even took a perverse pride in the fact that he had never needed anyone to complete his life. He certainly wanted no emotional entanglements. So why in hell was he thinking like some maudlin social worker about a child he hadn't known existed two weeks ago?

He stood up abruptly, startling Jenny.

"You're leaving?" she asked, surprised into displaying disappointment.

He shook his head, striding down to the water. He needed something to cool him off. He stopped abruptly and turned back to Jenny. "Why don't you ever go into the water?"

"I can't swim," she answered simply.

His face darkened alarmingly. "Wear a bathing suit tomorrow," he ordered. "I'll teach you."

She lowered her eyes, shamed color flooding her face. "I . . . I don't have one," she stammered miserably.

He muttered something obscene under his breath. To bring a child to a tropical island—and not even buy her a bathing suit! He turned and plunged into the surf, striking out with furious strokes.

Jenny gazed after him, a worried frown on her face. What had she done to make him so angry?

Steve smiled indulgently at Jenny's small, sodden figure as she padded happily ahead of him to where they'd thrown their towels. It hadn't been as onerous a chore as he had imagined, teaching Jenny the rudiments of swimming. After he'd impulsively sent the swimsuit to her by a maid last night, he'd berated himself for being a meddling fool. After all, what business was it of his if the child couldn't swim? He'd never done anything in his life so quixotic! Good Lord, what a sentimental gesture. He was thoroughly annoyed with himself. Still he'd arrived early at the beach this morning, and when he saw Jenny's radiant face, he knew he was lost. He felt such tenderness surge through him that his throat had tightened achingly.

He picked up a towel and tossed it to her. "Dry off," he said, looking at the wet, sleek hair clinging to her head. "You look like a seal, though you certainly don't swim like one," he added teasingly.

She smiled serenely. "I'll get better," she assured him.

"Yes, I believe you will," he replied, recalling her quiet stubbornness as she'd struggled desperately to follow his instructions.

He dried off briskly, spread his towel on the sand, and sat down. He watched idly for a few minutes as Jenny carefully pulled her hair over one shoulder, and dried it with her towel. Her face was solemn as she sat down beside him.

He took the towel away from her. "You have a smudge on your arm. I'll wipe it off."

She scooted away, and quickly reached for the towel. "That's all right," she said hurriedly. She draped the towel around her shoulders, and asked with an eager smile, "How long do you think it will take me to learn to swim as well as you?"

His eyes narrowed suspiciously as he gazed at her for a long moment. Then, without answering, he reached out and pulled the towel away from her shoulders.

"My God!"

He took her thin arm in his hand and turned it over to examine the four dark blemishes on the satiny skin. She sat resignedly as he did the same to the other arm, tracing the identical marks with a gentle finger. She didn't look at him, but when he released her, she silently took back the towel and continued to dry her hair.

"Who did it?" Steve asked harshly. He'd thought he'd become callous to the cruelties of life. He'd suffered enough curses and blows himself, growing up as an orphan in the slums of west side New York. But somehow the sight of the bruises on that delicate arm made him feel physically ill.

"They don't hurt," Jenny said evasively, her eyes fixed on a point beyond Jason's shoulder.

"Damn it, Jenny, answer me!" he demanded. "Who did that to you?"

She remained stubborn and silent, though her face was now tight and pale.

Steve cursed softly. He knew who had done it. Who else could it be but Jenny's father? He also knew that Jenny would never admit it. She had a core of loyalty that extended even to that bastard. She would simply sit there, looking miserably unhappy and not replying to any questions until he dropped the subject. It had happened before, but he couldn't let this particular subject drop.

"If it was your father, Jenny, tell me," he urged. "I'll find a way to protect you." His gaze was forcefully commanding.

She shook her head, but her silver eyes moved back to his face. "You mustn't do that," she said quietly. "It probably won't happen again. He was upset because he thought I'd asked you for the swimsuit." With a lithe movement, she was on her feet and then swiftly running down the sandy beach toward the distant hotel.

Steve gazed after her, his face grim. He shouldn't have pursued it, but he'd been driven to it by an almost uncontrollable anger at Cashman. When he'd seen those marks and known who'd inflicted them, he'd felt a savage, killing rage greater than any he'd ever known.

He illogically felt that Cashman had damaged something of his own. Sweet, solemn Jenny. His Jenny. He reached for his shirt lying beside the towel and extracted a pack of cigarettes. He lit one and inhaled deeply. Damn it, he hadn't felt as helpless as this since he was a small child. He was outraged that he should be so vulnerable to another human being.

After almost thirty years of being totally free of the weakness that attended caring for another person, he had been caught in an impossible situation. Somehow Jenny had crept under his guard and become important to him.

From the beginning he'd felt a strange affinity to the waif and now the emotion had grown until he had to acknowledge it. Whenever he was around the child, he felt a protective tenderness utterly foreign to him. He'd always been a realist of the first order, but he was aware of something that was almost a little mystical in his affection for Jenny. He sometimes had the odd sensation she'd been waiting all her life for him to turn around and see her sitting by that sand castle with that grave, endearing look on her face. It was ironic that the one person who had penetrated his iron reserve was only a child. Worse, a child under the guardianship of a man who not only neglected her, but was actually brutal to her.

He crushed the cigarette out in the sand in a burst of frustration. If Jenny had been the pampered, beloved child of doting parents, the situation would have been completely different. He would have acknowledged that he had no place in her life, but Cashman's treatment of Jenny nullified any rights to her in Steve's eyes. He would have no scruples in removing Jenny from Cashman's influence, but the problem it posed was enormous.

He frowned thoughtfully as he stood up and slipped on his shirt. He picked up the towels, slinging them over one shoulder as he started to walk slowly back to the hotel. His blue eyes were narrowed as his facile brain turned over the possibilities with computerlike rapidity.

It would be difficult, but he'd never yet failed in accomplishing a goal once he had resolved it was worth attaining. Now that he had admitted that

something must be done about young Jenny Cashman, the result was already a foregone conclusion
as far as he was concerned. He had only to deter-
mine his course of action.

"The doctor said it was probably a heart attack,"
Joe Magruder said casually. In his experience it
wasn't uncommon for a man to die in the casino.
Tension ran high at times, and a heart attack, while
regrettable, was not that unusual.

What was, however, was Steve Jason's keen interest in the matter. The casino manager had gone to
his employer's office as a mere matter of form. He
could have handled the details himself, but Steve
liked to be advised of all irregularities in the smooth
operation of his hotels.

After Steve had heard the name Henry Cashman,
though, his questions had been searching and bul-
let hard. Magruder wondered if Steve had actually
known Cashman. It was hardly likely; he seldom
concerned himself with the actual running of the
casino, and Henry Cashman was strictly in the
minor leagues.

That Steve Jason was definitely in the majors had been evident to Magruder when Jason had hired him away from a casino in Nassau to manage his new acquisition on Santa Flores. He had known powerful, dynamic men before, but Jason was exceptional. He was brilliant, charismatic, and the toughest bastard Magruder had ever run across. Little was known about his background, other than he was born in New York and raised in a series of orphanages and foster homes. After such a start in life, the fact that he was the owner of several hotels and casinos and hadn't yet turned thirty was not only remarkable, but phenomenal.

"I'll arrange to have the body transported to the magistrates in Nassau," Magruder went on briskly. "He had a British passport, and he evidently was a professional gambler." He made a face. "We accepted several of his markers. I guess we might just as well write them off as a loss." He added as an afterthought, "He has a kid of about nine staying with him at the hotel."

"Eleven," Steve corrected absently.

"What?"

"His daughter is eleven."

So Steve Jason did have some connection with Cashman. "I figured we'd turn the kid over to the authorities in Nassau," Magruder said casually. "They can keep her in a welfare center there until they locate possible relatives."

"No!" The word shot out with involuntary violence, and Steve drew a deep steadying breath. Magruder's pragmatic suggestion regarding Jenny filled him with unreasoning rage. Steve knew from experience what orphanages were like, and the thought of Jenny in one made him sick.

The news of Cashman's death had shocked him strangely. Only yesterday he'd been thinking what a bloody bastard he must be, and now the man was dead. There was no need for the tentative plans he'd made to rescue young Jenny. It was enough to make one believe in fate. Never had something he wanted fallen so easily into his hands. The child was alone. No, she was free, he amended. He would see that she would never be alone.

"We'll keep her here until they locate someone," he said. "Tell the desk clerk she's to stay in the same room. She'd better have someone with her, so tell housekeeping that Esmeralda is to move in with her temporarily."

"Esmeralda?" Magruder asked in bewilderment.

"She's one of our maids," Steve said impatiently, rising to his feet.

Magruder rose also, his mind a jumble of speculation. "The kid hasn't been told yet. Shall we wait until morning and have this Esmeralda tell her?"

Steve shook his head. "I'll tell her myself. And I'll tell her tonight. Have someone wake her and bring her down here to the office." Then as Magruder went to the door he added, "And make sure they don't frighten her!"

Magruder left, shaking his head in amazement. Steve Jason was hard as a diamond, and Magruder would have laid odds that he didn't give a damn about anyone in the world. A Steve Jason capable of caring whether a child was frightened was outside his experience.

When Jenny was brought into the office by a bustling and intensely curious maid, she was dressed as always in shorts and shirt. Jason wondered with obscure indignation if she had any other clothes. Her eyes that had been cloudy with sleep and bewilderment, widened with surprise and delight at the sight of him behind the large desk.

She came forward, smiling happily. "The maid said the owner of the hotel wanted to see me. Do you own the Santa Flores, Steve?"

He nodded, wondering how to start. "Does that surprise you?" he asked, thinking how readily she adapted. She accepted being dragged out of bed in the middle of the night as a matter of course—and it probably *was* with a father like Henry Cashman.

"Not really," she said thoughtfully. "You look like you should run things."

He shrugged. He'd never had any use for people who beat around the bush when unpleasant facts were to be told. "I have bad news for you, Jenny," he said bluntly. "Your father died tonight."

Her silver eyes widened in shock and the small face whitened. He felt the same swift rage he'd known yesterday, that anything should hurt her. She was so little.

She sat down in the chair beside the desk, her face a mask of disbelief.

"I'm sorry, Jenny," he said. "It was a heart attack. It was very quick; he didn't suffer."

"I'm supposed to cry, aren't I?" she asked numbly. "He was my father, I'm supposed to cry."

He felt an unfamiliar lump in his throat. "Grief affects people in different ways, Jenny. Tears are only one of them."

Her eyes flew to his, and he was shocked at the desolation in them. "He didn't like me, you know." Her voice was husky. "I got in his way."

Again came that tide of anger. Henry Cashman must have been even more of a bastard than he'd believed. "How would you like to continue living here for a little while, Jenny?" he asked briskly. "Until the authorities can find your next of kin?"

The gray eyes were suddenly filled with hope. "Could I do that? They won't make me leave right away?"

"No one will make you do anything that you don't want to do."

"Then I want to stay on at Santa Flores," she said. "With you, Steve."

The sea was smooth as sapphire silk this morning, caressing the shore with a gentle frill of white lace. Steve stood waiting impatiently, his hands on his hips as he watched Jenny walking slowly along the beach from the hotel. His eyes narrowed on her face that was definitely troubled, and his own expression darkened in a frown. It had been only four months and already he felt as if she were a part of him. Her distress communicated itself to him effortlessly, and for the first time in his life he knew he was nakedly vulnerable to another human being.

"It must have taken you ten minutes to walk down from the hotel," he said mockingly when she finally reached him. "I've seen you make it in two. What's the matter? Feeling your age, old lady?"

"I've got something to tell you," she said, her gray eyes sober.

He arched a brow. "Before we swim?" Usually Jenny couldn't wait to get into the water. She'd taken to swimming like a dolphin.

She nodded seriously.

He spread the towel and sat down, patting the place beside him. "So sit down and tell me."

"Esmeralda says you're spending a lot of money trying to find out who my relatives are," she said quickly, not looking at him. "She says you've hired a private investigator."

"Esmeralda is, as usual, very well informed." He noted the shadow of her lashes on her cheek. Why was the child so upset? "I gather she didn't find that out from Joe, the fisherman."

"No, from your secretary." Jenny twisted her hands in agitation.

"I can afford the money, Jenny," he said gently. "Don't worry about it."

"But you shouldn't have to," she burst out miserably. "It's no use. They're not going to find anyone who wants me."

He went still, his eyes keen and watchful. "Why do you say that?"

She looked up, her eyes pleading. "I'm sorry. I should have told you before. I just didn't want to go away."

"Told me what, Jenny?" he asked patiently. "You haven't told me anything as yet."

She drew a deep breath. "Once when my father was angry, he told me that he'd never have put up with having me with him if he could have gotten rid of me. He tried to get my mother's people to take me after my mother died when I was born. They refused."

"Charming," Steve muttered savagely. The more he heard about Henry Cashman, the more he was convinced the world was better off without him.

"You have a right to be angry," she said in a low voice. "I should have told you right away. I just wanted to spend a little more time here." She drew a shaky breath. "They're not going to find anyone, so you might as well stop paying that detective and turn me over to those welfare people in Nassau."

"Jenny, I received a complete report from the detective agency two months ago," he murmured. "I've known for some time that you had no one to go to."

Her eyes widened. "Then why am I still here? Why haven't you sent me away?"

He reached out and brushed a strand of dark silky hair behind her ear. "I wanted you to get used to me. I wanted you to feel at ease on Santa Flores."

She was silent, her eyes questioning.

He ran a hand through his dark gold hair, frowning impatiently. "I don't know how in the hell to say this," he said gruffly. "I've never had a family, so I don't know how to act like a father or a brother to you. I'll probably be terrible at it. But I care about you, and I don't want you to go away. If you like, perhaps we could be friends." It was a strangely awkward speech for someone who was usually so facile with words. To Jenny it sounded beautiful.

The tears rushed to her eyes. "Oh, yes," she said brokenly. "Oh, yes, please."

He grinned. "I'm glad you agree. I had the court in Nassau make you my ward three weeks ago."

Her smile was blinding in its radiance. "Then it's all settled?" she asked excitedly. "I belong to you?"

He felt a strange shock of pleasure at hearing that phrase. He took her small hand in his. "Yes," he said. "You belong to me, Jenny."

Two

"I WOULD LIKE to see Mr. Jason, please."

Pat Marchant looked up from the document in front of her with an absent smile. Her eyes widened. The girl before her was perhaps fourteen, clad in a navy blue skirt and a loose blazer jacket that was obviously a school uniform. Her long black hair was tied with a navy blue band. Her face was innocent of makeup, and she had the most extraordinarily beautiful gray eyes that Pat had ever seen.

"I'm afraid that won't be possible," she said, not unkindly, wondering idly if the girl was collecting for some school organization. Steve Jason, as owner of one of the largest and most luxurious casino hotels on the Las Vegas strip, was always being solicited for contributions of some kind. "Mr. Jason is out for the day. Perhaps I could help you."

Jenny bit her lip in disappointment. She should have known that she couldn't just walk in and see Steve, but would have to get around some protective dragon. This one didn't seem so bad, though. She had a nice smile.

"Pat, I've brought the cash receipts." The voice behind her was blessedly familiar, and Jenny whirled and threw herself into the arms of the short, spare man, who instinctively caught her with one arm while rescuing the metal box he was holding with the other.

"Oh, Joe, I'm so glad to see you! I didn't know what to do," Jenny said.

Joe Magruder stared in blank amazement at her. "Jenny? What on earth are you doing here? I thought you were still in school in Switzerland." His shrewd, cynical brown eyes stared suspiciously into Jenny's. "Does Steve know you're here?"

Jenny shook her head tiredly. "I left Madame

Junot's yesterday morning and I've been traveling ever since."

"A kid like you traipsing around Europe by yourself? Steve is *not* going to be pleased," Joe said grimly.

"Oh, Joe, for goodness sake, I'm nineteen!" she said in exasperation.

Joe did some rapid calculations, then shook his head in amazement. "That's right, you must be, but you sure don't look it."

"I know," she said in disgust. "I'm ridiculously small." She brightened. "But I have filled out a bit in the last year."

He cast a skeptical look at the tiny figure in the shapeless navy uniform.

"I have," she insisted. "You can't tell in this thing." She flicked a contemptuous hand at the lapels of her blazer and made a wry face. "I assure you I was quite safe the entire trip. The only attention girls like me get are from little old ladies trying to mother them."

"I'm not so sure about that," he said slowly. The thin pointed face he was looking into was not conventionally pretty, but its fine bone structure and well defined features were compelling and fascinating. God knows her eyes were magnificent—clear crystal gray, almost silver, framed by extravagantly long black lashes.

"Well, I am," she said gloomily, then added more urgently, "I've got to see Steve, Joe. Where is he?"

"I don't know, Jenny." He turned to the secretary who had been silent through the exchange, dazed bewilderment on her face. "Pat?"

"He's in San Francisco checking out some real estate," the red-haired secretary replied quickly. "He should be back later this afternoon."

"I'd better take you upstairs to the apartment," Joe said. "Where are your bags?"

Jenny pointed to the single flight bag on the floor beside her.

"That's all?" he asked, his eyebrows raised in surprise.

"That's all," she affirmed cheerfully, picking up the bag and slipping the strap over her shoulder.

Joe turned to the secretary, and handed her the metal strongbox he'd been carrying. "When Steve comes in, ask him to call me, will you?" She nodded, still staring avidly at Jenny. "And Pat," her glance moved back to him as he paused, "don't tell him about the kid."

With his hand under her elbow, Joe escorted Jenny into the elevator and pushed the button for the penthouse. Jenny leaned wearily against the wall of the elevator. Everything was suddenly strange and bewildering. When she had made the decision to leave school and come to Las Vegas, it had all seemed so clearcut and simple, but the sight of the Santa Flores Hotel had dazzled and intimidated her. She suddenly straightened her shoulders and squared her chin firmly. Why should she let this beautiful monolith of a hotel intimidate her? Heaven knows she'd been dragged through enough of them before she'd come under Steve's care. Just because she'd become accustomed to the security blanket Steve had enfolded her in for the last eight years was no reason for her to forget the hardy little gypsy she'd been before he'd come into her life.

"Why did he call it the Santa Flores?" she asked abruptly.

Joe Magruder shrugged. "Who knows why Steve does anything? He's never really had a homebase. He probably stayed on Santa Flores longer than anywhere else. Maybe he's a bit sentimental about it." There was a distinct note of skepticism in Magruder's voice. In his association with his employer, he'd rarely known him to act out of sentiment—the singular exception being his relationship with Jenny.

The elevator stopped, and Jenny followed Magruder to the door immediately opposite it.

"Mike won't be in at this time of day, he's always down at the pool girlwatching," Joe said dryly, pulling a key chain from his pocket. "That's why Steve gave me a key to the place."

"Mike's here, too?" Jenny was delighted. "I thought he was still on Santa Flores."

Joe shook his head as he pushed the door open. "Steve pulled us both out of there when he opened this hotel." Turning left at the foyer, he said, "Come on along to the kitchen and I'll make you a sandwich. You look as though you could use it."

Jenny trailed behind him to the ultramodern kitchen. Her gaze ran admiringly over the stainless steel appliances and the copper pots and pans hanging over the central butcher block work area.

"Mike must be in heaven," she said.

"It's his pride and joy," Joe admitted. "Steve let Mike design the kitchen when he had the interior decorator in to do the apartment." He opened the refrigerator door. "Sit down and relax."

Jenny collapsed gratefully into one of the scarlet leather kitchen chairs at the chrome table, sighing with relief. She took a measure of comfort that Mike would be here soon. It was Mike Novacek who had helped her to adjust to her new life on Santa Flores eight years ago; maybe he could perform the same magic here.

Mike had been in his early twenties then, an ex-navy cook, who, after his hitch in the service, was too restless to settle down. He had ended up on Santa Flores working as a bouncer in Steve Jason's casino by virtue of his truly formidable physique. When Steve discovered the burly ex-sailor had a passion for cooking and a talent that was indeed extraordinary, he had made him combination cook-companion-bodyguard for Jenny. Esmeralda had recently married her fisherman and moved to the other side of the island, so Jenny was put into Mike's care. It had been a wise choice. Filled with a boundless joie de vivre, Mike loved cooking, girls, and the good life in that order, and he had treated Jenny like a beloved little sister until Steve had decided she should go away to school.

Joe set a sandwich and a glass of milk before Jenny and sat down opposite her. "Eat," he ordered gently.

She picked up the sandwich and took a bite. It was ham and cheese and tasted delicious after the plastic meals she'd had on the plane. She ate it greedily and pushed the empty plate away with a satisfied sigh.

Joe Magruder had been waiting patiently until she'd finished. "Now," he said, "don't you think you'd better tell me why you're here? I can't help you with Steve unless I know what I'm facing."

"I'm nineteen," Jenny said quietly. "I've been at Madame Junot's for six years. I decided it was time I stopped taking advantage of Steve's generosity. I'm going to get a job."

"Uh-uh." Joe shook his head. "No way."

Jenny raised her chin. "We'll see. I'm not going back to Madame Junot's."

"Perhaps you could go to some other school."

"In his last letter Steve said he was sending me to college in Paris next quarter."

"Well, there you are. It's settled."

Jenny shook her head. "I'm not letting him pay for another four years of education when I can support myself perfectly well now. He's been too generous to me as it is."

"He doesn't think of it as generosity, Jenny," Joe said with conviction. "He cares about you. Steve's a funny guy and he's always been a loner. When he made you his ward, you could have knocked me over with a feather. But I watched him with you. You're important to him. You may be the only person who is."

"Do you know that I haven't seen him in almost two years?" she asked tautly. "How important can I be?"

"He's been awfully busy, Jenny. The Santa Flores is a major project. He was working day and night for a year before it opened."

"It's been open six months," she pointed out, not looking at him.

"Oh, Jenny! It's not as if he's been neglecting you."

She looked up, her eyes bright with unshed tears. "Do you think I'm complaining about him? He doesn't owe me anything. He's been wonderful to me. For years every holiday he's taken me to the most wonderful places. He writes to me. He calls me now and then just to see if everything is all right. He's the perfect older brother."

"Well, then?" Joe asked, frankly puzzled.

"He gives me everything," she said desperately. "I've grown to depend on him too much. How can I have any self-respect if I keep taking from him without giving anything in return?"

"But he doesn't want you to give him anything in return," Joe protested.

"I know." She drew a shaky breath and smiled sadly. "But I'm a person who needs to give, so we're at an impasse."

She quickly finished her milk, then stood, rinsed her glass and plate at the sink and put them in the drainer to dry. She turned back to Joe, who was watching her with a troubled expression, and smiled cheerfully. "Are you going to help me, Joe?" she coaxed sweetly. "I'll need all the support I can get when Steve finds out I'm here."

He rose to his feet. "I'll do my best. But you're the only one who has ever really had any influence with Steve. I think you're going to have to handle this one yourself." He picked up her flight bag. "Come on, I'll show you the guest room."

The bedroom he led her to was in perfect taste, faultlessly decorated in Mediterranean decor with blues and greens predominating in the color scheme.

"There's an adjoining bath," Joe said, gesturing to a closed door. "Why don't you try to nap?"

"I will," she promised. "Thanks for everything, Joe."

"It's nothing, kid," he said lightly, with a farewell salute.

It wasn't nothing. Joe Magruder had always been kind to her in his quiet, rather cynical way. He was completely loyal to Steve Jason, and had extended the same loyalty to her as Steve's dependent.

Reaching up, she took the navy headband off and ran her fingers sensuously through her hair, then slipped off her jacket. Dropping her flight bag on the bed and unzipping it, she drew out underthings, a pair of faded jeans and a pale pink sun top. Leaving the jeans and top on the bed, she placed the underthings in a drawer in the bureau. Then crossing back to the bed, she took out the framed picture of Steve and placed it on the table beside the bed.

It was not a very good picture. She had taken it with the camera Steve had given her on one of their holiday jaunts, and she'd had it blown up and framed out of the generous allowance he sent her each month. It had been taken at Delphi on board a cruise ship almost three years ago, and Steve was leaning against the rail of the ship, dressed in fitted dark slacks and a bulky knit white sweater. The sea breeze had ruffled the dark gold of his hair and his lips were curved in his familiar mocking smile while the brilliant blue eyes gleamed derisively from the tough, good looking face. The picture had occupied the place of honor beside her bed at Madame Junot's for the past two years. She smiled reminiscently as she recalled that, poor as the picture was, it had received bedazzled attention from her schoolmates whose envious comments on her guardian had ranged from dreamy to downright sexy.

She headed for the shower, stripping off her clothes along the way. She turned on the water, tested it briefly, and stepped under the warm spray. Why did traveling always make one feel so grimy? She stayed there a long time, shampooing her long dark hair and rinsing it carefully.

Wrapping one towel around her hair and another around her body, she went back into the bedroom. She stared longingly at the wide bed, then shook her head determinedly. Her hair would be a mess if she didn't care for it at once. She used the blow dryer she'd found in the bathroom, and then brushed the dark locks vigorously. She'd been tempted to have her hair cut many times, but she felt it was her one asset. The long, shiny mane fell like a thick curtain to the middle of her back, turning under slightly on the ends. She had cut a fringe of bangs last summer, and it gave her a satisfyingly exotic look, she thought happily.

Not that she was even in the same league with the gorgeous beauties Steve always had in tow. She had realized soon after she'd come to live on Santa Flores that Steve was a very virile man who had a magnetic attraction for women. She remembered ruefully how jealous she'd been at the attention he'd given them, but she'd soon realized that they were never permanent fixtures. He used them casually and when bored, took another to his bed. She doubted that Steve even knew how painful she'd found his affairs. He'd been meticulously careful about keeping his life with her a thing apart, but Santa Flores was a small resort town, and Mike Novacek had never been reticent about commenting cheerfully on Steve's women.

Jenny shook her head angrily. She'd thought she'd gotten over comparing herself to Steve's mistresses years ago. He would never even think of her in that light. She was the little sister, the companion, family. She occupied a special place in Steve Jason's life and she ought to accept that gracefully. With that stern self-admonition, she pulled back the magnificent turquoise spread on the bed and slipped between the sheets. She was asleep in minutes.

When Jenny awoke, the last golden rays of the sun were filtering through the drawn turquoise drapes, bathing the room in a tranquil blue haze like a chamber at the bottom of the sea. She lazily turned her head toward the clock on the bedside table, and then sat up hurriedly. It was after seven and she'd slept almost four hours! She swung quickly to her feet and set about getting dressed. Steve would no doubt be arriving soon, and she'd been hoping for a few minutes to greet Mike before she had to face her guardian. She quickly dressed in her faded jeans, which fit snugly over her hips, and slipped into the pink top. She didn't bother with a bra. She'd outgrown all the ones she owned last summer, and had gotten used to the comfortable freedom she enjoyed without one. Looking into the mirror, she bit her lips uncertainly. The suntop was lower than she remembered, and the knit material clung revealingly to her high, full breasts. She shrugged. Oh well, it was this or the uniform, and the latter was definitely soiled. She tidied her hair hurriedly and made her way to the kitchen to greet Mike.

She found him standing at the stove dressed in an elegant blue short-sleeved pullover, tight black pants and Gucci loafers. His only concession to his culinary duties was the white towel wrapped casually around his waist.

"Mike!" Jenny cried happily, launching herself at him.

He spun around, a wide grin on his face, catching her and swinging her boisterously in a circle. "Little Jenny!" he said. "Joe told me you'd arrived."

"Mike, you haven't changed at all," she said breathlessly when he finally put her down.

"I'm just better looking."

No one could ever call him good looking, Jenny thought lovingly. He stood over six feet, with a powerful frame and muscular biceps that were truly intimidating. The craggy, rough-hewn face with its broken nose and small scar at the corner of one eye was mean and tough looking, even in repose. However, there was almost always a genial, breezy grin on his face and a twinkle in the hazel eyes that reflected his supreme zest for living.

His eyes went over her appraisingly and his eyebrows shot up in surprise. "Still five foot nothing," he announced dryly, his eyes on the cleavage revealed by the pink top. "But *you've* definitely changed, chicken!"

Jenny blushed, hiking the straps of the suntop higher. "I'm so glad you're here, Mike," she said, her eyes warm. "Do you like it as much as you liked Santa Flores?"

"Who wouldn't?" he asked, grinning. "Easy job, good pay, and Las Vegas show girls. I'd be crazy not to be happy."

"*Still* chasing girls, Mike?"

"My favorite sport," he admitted, turning back to the stove to stir a delicious smelling concoction. "Do you realize that Las Vegas has more show girls than anywhere else in the country? All quite gorgeous, too." He made a face. "Of course, quite a few try to use me to get to Steve." He shrugged philosophically. "That's okay with me. A man can be pretty happy with Steve's leftovers."

A frown clouded Jenny's forehead. "Is Steve here yet?"

"He's in the hotel," Mike said softly, glancing knowingly at her worried face. "Pat called to tell me he was going to Joe's office."

He lifted a saucepan from the flame and set it on a back burner. "You know he's not going to like this little surprise of yours."

"Too bad," she said flippantly. She wished everyone would stop saying that. She was nervous enough without Joe's and now Mike's warning.

"He sent you away to school because he thought his life style wasn't healthy for a young kid," Mike said shortly. "Do you think he's going to risk his innocent little ward in a wild town like Las Vegas?" He shook his head. "Not likely, chicken. Steve's much too protective." Then, seeing the downcast expression on her face, he softened. "Oh, hell! I didn't mean to make you unhappy, Jenny. I'm making all of Steve's favorite dishes tonight. I figured it might soothe the savage breast, so to speak. Knowing Steve, that could be like trying to tame Big Foot by offering him a snowcone."

She smiled. "How is he, Mike? Has he changed?"

From the corner of her eye she saw him shrug. "A little maybe," he said thoughtfully. "He's harder and tougher, maybe a bit more cynical than he was at Santa Flores. That goes with the territory, I guess. He's really rich now, powerful, too. But he hasn't changed in the way he feels about you, Jenny."

Her silver eyes flew back to his. "How can you be so sure? It's been a long time."

There was a curiously undecided look in Mike's hazel eyes before he evidently came to a decision. "Come on," he said abruptly. "I want to show you something." Taking her by the hand, he pulled her along behind him through the apartment and into what was obviously the master bedroom. "This is Steve's room," he announced.

It was as beautifully decorated as the room she'd been given, Jenny thought. It had the same look of opulence, but the lush carpet was pearl gray, and the spread on the king-sized bed was black shot with subtle touches of silver.

With his hands on her shoulders, Mike turned her around so that she was facing the wall beside the door. "Look!"

She caught her breath and her eyes widened in surprise.

It was not a large painting, perhaps only two feet square, but it had been beautifully executed and the artist had caught something ephemeral that made the subject come brilliantly alive. It was a small girl sitting quietly in the sand, her long dark silky hair blowing gently in the breeze, while her strange silver eyes looked out of the painting with a serenity that was both quaint and infinitely moving. There was a half-built sand castle before her.

"Why, it's me!" Jenny said incredulously. "But how?"

"Steve was in Carmel last fall looking at some investment property, when he ran across a small gift shop that featured the works of local artists," Mike explained, his gaze fixed admiringly on the painting. "He was very impressed by one of the paintings. It was the portrait of an old fisherman, and it seemed to see beyond the flesh to the soul." Mike looked a trifle embarrassed. "At least, that's what Steve said.

"He discovered the portrait had been painted by a young artist named Joel Whiting, who rented a rundown cottage on the beach. He contacted the artist and offered to give him a show at one of the finest galleries in Southern California if he would paint a portrait of you from a color photograph he'd taken years ago on Santa Flores." Mike shook his head in amazement. "The idiot almost turned it down. He was all full of ideals and theories about the purity of his art. He didn't want to copy a photograph like some hack artist in a shopping mall."

He shrugged. "Anyway, Steve persuaded him to do it, and the painting has been hanging there ever since."

"It's a wonderful painting," Jenny said throatily, her eyes glistening. "Thank you for showing it to me, Mike."

He grinned, his hazel eyes gentle. "I don't think Steve would have gone to such a hell of a lot of trouble to get that painting done if he had changed toward you. Do you, chicken?"

Jenny shook her head slowly, feeling a wave of warm contentment surge over her. "No, I guess he wouldn't."

"Right," Mike said briskly. "Now I've got to get cracking." He headed for the door, and said over his shoulder, "Why don't you go into the living room and play the stereo. Something nice and *soothing!*"

She followed his advice. The sunken living room was as lovely as the rest of the apartment, with a long, lush velvet couch and deep easy chairs in rich burgundy, and white area rugs over the polished inlaid wood flooring. She flicked on a lamp and put a record on the stereo. Cautiously following Mike's suggestion, she chose Debussy. Then sinking down on the couch, she curled up in one corner, resting her head on the arm. She closed her eyes and let the music drain the tension from her rigid muscles.

"Jenny!"

The angry voice was belovedly familiar, and she leaped to her feet and was across the room in seconds. She flew into Steve's arms like a homing pigeon. Those arms enfolded her automatically, then as she nestled closer, they tightened for a brief moment before pushing her firmly away.

"Steve," she whispered happily, her face lit up as if with the warmth of the morning sun. "It's been such a long time." She hid her face in his shirt, breathing in the lovely male smell of him.

"Too long, evidently," he said tightly, pushing her away again. His blue eyes narrowed. "You used to know better than to disobey orders, Jenny."

Her eyes filled with tears. "Aren't you glad to see me?"

His expression was angry for a moment. Then he sighed and pulled her back into his arms for a quick hug. "You know I am," he said gruffly, kissing her gently on the tip of her nose. "But that's not going to let you off the hook, young lady."

"I know," she whispered, nestling closer and smiling mischievously. "It never did, but it makes me feel better."

He stared down at her bemusedly, then shook his head. Slipping an arm around Jenny's slim waist, he led her back into the living room, settling himself beside her on the couch. He took a cigarette out of the carved teak box on the coffee table and lit it, drawing in the smoke with an almost sensual enjoyment. Then he turned back to regard her lazily.

"My God! What have you got on?" he exclaimed sharply, his eyes on the front of the pink top. She pulled ineffectually at the neckline, wishing miserably that she'd worn the uniform blouse, soiled or not.

"You're just making it worse," he snapped. "Another minute and you'll fall out of it entirely! Where the hell did you get a thing like that?"

"You bought it for me," she said defensively. "Two years ago, in Athens. Don't you remember?"

"*I* bought you that thing?"

She shrugged uncomfortably. "It looks different now. I've grown."

"Obviously. I suggest you go change into something a little less revealing before we go in to dinner."

"I haven't got anything else," she said. "Only my school uniform, and I've worn that for nearly two days." She grimaced distastefully.

"I'm glad you traveled light," he said grimly. "You won't have to bother with luggage when I send you back tomorrow."

"I didn't have any choice about that," she admitted, not looking at him.

"What do you mean?"

"I sold all my clothes."

"You what?" he exploded.

"I had a dormitory sale," she said with cheerful bravado. "You have terrific taste, Steve. Everything was snatched up right away."

His mouth was a thin line as he enunciated his words with careful precision. "Would it be too much to ask why you sold your entire wardrobe to your giggling school friends?"

"I had to," she said simply. "I didn't have enough left from my allowance for the air fare. Even after the sale, I didn't have quite enough. I had to hitch-hike to Zurich."

"You hitchhiked?" he echoed with soft menace.

"I got a lift from a farmer and his wife," she interjected hurriedly. "It was perfectly safe." She was aware of the frozen fury in his face. "I wouldn't have sold the clothes you gave me if I hadn't out-grown them anyway," she assured him desperately. "I've grown quite a lot this last year."

"I've noticed," he bit out. "You little idiot! Do you know the risk you ran? Anything could have happened to you. You could have been murdered or raped, and all because of some harebrained scheme!"

"Joe told you?" She moistened her lips nervously.

"You're damn right. I've never heard of such an asinine idea in my life. You're far too young to be on your own. You're going back to school."

"I'm not going back," she said, her gray eyes steady. "There are lots of girls my age supporting themselves. I'm not taking any more from you, Steve."

"For God's sake, you're only nineteen," he said with exasperation, running his hand through the dark gold of his hair. "What kind of job can you get without some kind of training?"

She grimaced and leaned back on the couch. "You have a point," she admitted. "Madame Junot's Academy wasn't long on vocational training. I can't even type."

"Well, then go to college," Steve said, pouncing swiftly. "A few years there and you'd come out qualified to support yourself, if that's what you want."

She shook her head again. "I'm not letting you support me any longer," she said obstinately. "I'll wait on tables if I have to, and go to school at night."

"The hell you will."

"Yes, the hell I *will*."

Suddenly his face changed, the anger replaced by a warm smile that was designed to melt all opposition. It usually succeeded, she thought despairingly, feeling her resistance ebb away as it always had in the past.

"Don't be silly, Jenny," he murmured, his hand caressing the dark silk of her hair. "I'm disgustingly rich these days. Let me give a little to you."

"You've given me quite a lot already. But it's time I stood on my own two feet." She paused. "Don't think I'm not grateful."

"I don't want your gratitude," Steve grated between his teeth, his smile gone. "I want you to behave sensibly."

"And do what you say," she finished softly.

"Right."

She leaned forward, her hands on his arms, her eyes pleading. "I can't do that. Not this time, Steve. I know the money doesn't mean anything to you, but it does to me. It means I'm not my own person."

He studied her distressed face for a long moment. "We'd better go in to dinner," he said suddenly. He rose and extended his hand to pull her to her feet. "And since you're not exactly formally dressed," he added, "I'd better get rid of this." He shrugged out of his navy blue jacket, discarded his tie, and rolled up his shirt sleeves to bare his tanned muscular forearms.

Impulsively she put her hand on his arm, loving his warm vitality. "Steve, you're not really angry with me?" she asked huskily, her silver eyes misty.

"Of course I'm angry with you," he said harshly. "What the hell have I been . . ." He broke off abruptly as his gaze met the hurt pleading in her own. For an instant his electric blue eyes retained their former flintiness, then they were glowing with warmth. His lips twisted wryly as he held out his arms. "Come here, brat," he ordered softly, and she flew contentedly into his embrace to be cradled there with loving gentleness. "One of these days I'm going to learn how to look into those big gray eyes without melting like a wax candle, and then you'll be in big trouble, young lady," he said, a suspicion of huskiness in his own voice. "Hell, do you think I want to send you back to school? You're the only family that I've ever had, baby." He was rocking her tenderly as if she were an infant. Jenny closed her eyes dreamily, feeling deliciously cosseted. "Sometimes I'm tempted to keep you with me regardless of what's best for you." He tilted her head back, framing her face with his hands and gazing down into her eyes with an expression that was oddly grave. "I've been a selfish bastard all my life, but I promised myself when you came to me that I'd always take care of you. Sometimes that means doing things that are rough on both of us. Can you understand that?"

Jenny turned her head and pressed her lips gently against the palm that was still cradling her cheek. "I understand," she said softly. "But you're wrong, Steve. I needed your protection when I was a child but I don't any more. I'm grown up now. You've got to let me go."

There was a flicker of pain on his face. He moved his palm from the softness of her lips and his index finger lightly traced their pink freshness. "Not yet," he said thickly. "I may have to let you go eventually, Jenny, but that time hasn't come yet." He drew a deep ragged breath and suddenly that strange vulnerability was gone from his face, replaced by his customary mockery. His hands dropped and he stepped back. "And until that time does arrive, you'll do exactly as I say." He gestured toward the door. "Dinner," he said firmly.

Steve appeared to have dismissed the subject, but Jenny knew him better than to believe that. He had only put it aside, to approach it later from a new line of attack. But she was grateful for the brief respite from hostilities. It always shattered her to be at odds with Steve.

There was little conversation during the excellent meal that Mike set before them. When Mike discreetly withdrew with a confidential wink at Jenny, she smiled involuntarily. Steve intercepted the exchange, and then appraising the elaborate meal preparations, raised an eyebrow quizzically.

"Am I being set up?" he asked.

"In the nicest possible way," Jenny said serenely, applying herself enthusiastically to the beef stroganoff.

Steve's lips twitched, then broke into a reluctant smile as he picked up his own fork.

It wasn't until they reached the coffee stage that he spoke again. "Suppose we give it two weeks," he suggested abruptly. "You haven't had a break from school for a long time. Take a little vacation and think things over. We'll talk about it again then."

She nodded eagerly, her face lighting magically. It was more of a concession than she'd expected to wrest from him.

"Don't think you've won, Jenny," Steve warned softly. "I've just postponed the inevitable. I'm still going to get my way in this." There was steely determination in the keen blue eyes.

She didn't answer, her glance falling before his.

"In the meantime," he went on briskly, "I think we'd better replenish your wardrobe. There are several excellent shops in the hotel. I'll leave word that you're to have what you want."

"Thank you," she replied. "I'll reimburse you as soon as I find work."

"You will not reimburse me," he said between clenched teeth.

"I won't accept them any other way," she said calmly. "It's either that or I wear this for the next two weeks." She touched the despised pink top lightly.

"That you will not do." He glared at the low neckline. Then he sighed impatiently. "Damn it, Jenny, why must you be so difficult?"

She remained stubbornly silent.

"Okay," Steve conceded wearily. "We'll talk about that in two weeks, too. *If* you get a job, we'll work something out."

Jenny smiled happily.

"There's cream on your whiskers, little kitten,"

he said, his eyes gleaming dangerously. "Remember, I gave you this victory, you didn't win it."

He stood up, dropping his white damask napkin beside his plate. "Now, as much as I've enjoyed our little passage of arms, I must leave you. I've plans for the evening. I'm sure you can entertain yourself."

"You're going out?"

"Your arrival was unexpected," he said coolly. "I'll see you in the morning, Jenny." He strode out of the room.

She wondered if he would have cancelled those plans if she hadn't defied him. He was upset with her and probably got a lot of satisfaction out of punishing her. And punishment it was. She rose from the table and trailed gloomily back to her room, speculating miserably on Steve's plans for the evening that more than likely included a beautiful woman.

THREE

JENNY WAS UP early the next morning, but when she entered the breakfast room she was disappointed to see that there was only one place setting.

Mike, entering with a plate of toast, observed her downcast face with a sympathetic grin. "He left about thirty minutes ago," he announced laconically, in answer to her unspoken question. "In a lousy temper, too. Sit down and I'll get you some breakfast."

"Can't I come into the kitchen with you?" Jenny asked, reluctant to sit in solitary splendor.

Mike hesitated a moment before shaking his head. "Best not, chicken. You're not a kid any-

Iris Johansen

more; Steve wouldn't like it." He disappeared into the kitchen and returned immediately with a plate of bacon and eggs, setting it before her with a flourish. "Any luck?" he asked curiously, pouring her orange juice.

"It was a stalemate," she answered. "We're giving it two weeks."

He whistled soundlessly. "You did better than I thought you would."

She bit into a piece of toast. "I've got to get a job, Mike," she said. "Do you have any suggestions?"

"Leave me out of it, Jenny," he said dryly. "I intend to keep the job I have."

"Coward," she charged, wrinkling her nose at him.

"You bet." He grinned. "Steve left a few messages for you." He enumerated them on his fingers. "One, he'll be busy all day, but will meet you at the Pagan Room for dinner at 8 p.m. Two, you're to go shopping. Three, when said shopping is done, you're to give me that pink blouse to burn."

She looked down at the top she wore again today. "Is it really that bad, Mike?" she asked.

His gaze fastened on the silky cleavage with fascination, then he pulled it away with no little effort and cleared his throat. "No, you're really a lovely thing, chicken, but Steve's pretty possessive about you. Much as he might like that sort of thing on someone else, you're still his little girl."

She finished the remainder of her orange juice, and stood up. "Only for the next two weeks," she said lightly. "Then I'm a woman on her own."

"We'll see," he drawled skeptically, vanishing once again into the kitchen.

Jenny made a face at the closed door. Mike was proving to be less than bolstering to her self-confidence. Well, they would all see that she meant what she said, she thought, squaring her shoulders. She strode purposefully to her bedroom to get her handbag, left the apartment, and took the elevator down to the lobby.

She spent the first half hour exploring the hotel with growing amazement. It was like a small city, containing several shops, numerous restaurants and nightclubs, and three swimming pools. The casino area was enormous, and was obviously the heart of the hotel. Even this early in the day the tables were crowded and doing a brisk business.

The entire complex had a tropical island theme, but she still couldn't associate it with her own Santa Flores.

Most of the guests in the lobby were casually but expensively dressed, she noted ruefully, and decided that it was time she visited the shops. The faded jeans she wore might be fashionable in student circles, but not here.

This fact was brought home to her clearly when she entered the largest boutique off the lobby. It was a fastidiously elegant shop. Thickly carpeted in soft rose with precisely matched rose walls, the decor made Jenny feel that she was enclosed in the heart of a flower. If such was the case, then the saleswoman who came gliding forward to greet her was surely an exotic butterfly.

Dressed smartly in pale green linen slacks and a cream tailored silk blouse, the attractive blonde gave off a positive aura of sophisticated elegance. The smile she gave Jenny was polite if a trifle reserved. The faded jeans again, Jenny realized.

"May I help you?" the blonde asked coolly.

Jenny nodded. "I hope so!" She grinned. "I obvi-

ously need all the help I can get. I'm Jenny Cashman."

The woman melted like an iceberg hitting the
equator. "Mr. Jason left word you'd be in today,"
she said warmly. "I'm Dinah James. I'm very happy
to meet you, Miss Cashman. Now, where shall we
start?"

They started from the inside and worked their
way out. Delicate lingerie, wispy night things,
lovely negligees. Then they went on to the elegant
day dresses, dress pants, blazers, skirts, and blouses.
Jenny would have stopped there, but Miss James
had her instructions. "Sports things," she said definitely. Jeans, chinos, tennis clothes, bathing suits.

"Now, an evening gown," the blonde said with
satisfaction. "I have just the one."

The gown was a drift of misty gray chiffon, fashioned in the Greek tradition and leaving one shoulder bare. It fell in fine pleats to the floor and was
bound under the breasts and at the waist with narrow silver cord. It clung to each curve lovingly and
was fantastically flattering to the clear silver of
Jenny's eyes. The clinging gown pointed up the
narrowness of her waist and accented the surpris-

ing fullness of her breasts. Why, she looked almost sexy in a classical way, Jenny thought happily.

"Gosh, that's gorgeous!" The exclamation was sincerely admiring, and the girl who uttered it was standing at the accessory counter with an alligator bag in her hand.

"It is, isn't it?" Jenny agreed blissfully, turning around to see the back in the full-length mirror.

"Pocket Venus," the girl announced suddenly, snapping her fingers.

"What?" Jenny asked, startled, turning back to her.

The other girl grinned. "I'm addicted to Regency romance novels. They used to refer to a girl with a figure like yours as a 'Pocket Venus.'"

Jenny made a face. "Now we're just called pint-sized."

Dinah James was unfastening the zipper of the gown with businesslike efficiency. "I think that's all that's necessary at the moment," she said briskly. "You can always come back if you find you need something else."

Jenny went into the dressing room, slipped out of the gown, and once again donned her faded denims and pink top. When she came out of the booth, she handed the gown to the sales assistant, who added it to the crowded wardrobe rack.

"I'll call the porter to take these up to Mr. Jason's apartment," Miss James said, straightening the gown on its hanger.

The girl at the accessory counter wandered over to look in awed admiration at the lovely clothes on the rack. "Jackpot!" she breathed ecstatically. "I've always wanted to go into a store and buy everything in sight. It's got to be every girl's dream. I'm Carol Morris," she introduced herself, turning to Jenny with a friendly smile. "From Los Angeles."

"Jenny Cashman," Jenny replied, liking the girl's casual warmth. Carol was about her own age, she thought. She had a sleek, glossy brown pageboy and lovely brown eyes. She was not particularly pretty, but had the attractiveness of glowing healthy skin, shining, well-styled hair, and a slim athletic body.

"You're staying with Mr. Jason?" Carol asked curiously.

Jenny nodded. "I'm his ward. Do you know Steve?"

"I should be so lucky! Gosh, he's a sexy hunk.

My father's presiding over the medical convention here, and we were introduced to Mr. Jason a few days ago. My brother was positively green with envy. He's been trying to cultivate that brand of rakish charm for years."

"I don't think it can be taught," Jenny said with a twinkle in her eyes. "It must be in the genes."

"Well, they ought to bottle it," Carol asserted. "Scott would be a steady customer."

"Scott is your brother?"

Carol nodded. "My older brother. He's a quarterback at UCLA. You've probably heard of him, Scott Morris?" She beamed in pride.

Jenny shook her head apologetically. "Quarterback? Is that football?"

The other girl stared at her, dumbfounded by such abysmal ignorance. "Gosh, yes," she exclaimed. "You mean you haven't heard of him? He's a sure thing to be drafted by the pros. All my friends are crazy about him."

"I've been in Switzerland for the past few years. I'm afraid I'm out of touch."

Carol immediately changed moods. "Switzerland! How terrific!" she cried. "My parents have promised to take us to Paris next summer. Have you been there?"

"Yes, three years ago. You'll love it," Jenny assured her.

Carol checked her wristwatch. "Oh, damn! I've got to meet my father and Scott for lunch. Look, I'd love to hear about Paris. Would it be all right if I called you? Maybe we could get together and chat. We'll be here for another week."

Jenny nodded. "I'll look forward to it."

With a smile and a wave of her hand, Carol hurried out of the boutique.

Jenny spent an additional thirty minutes at the shop choosing accessories and a deluxe makeup kit. Then, with sincere thanks to Dinah James, she left the boutique and took the elevator back up to the apartment. She went immediately to the kitchen, only to find it empty. Mike must be girl-watching again, she thought with amusement. By the time she'd made herself a sandwich and eaten it, there were two porters at the door with the wardrobe rack and a heap of boxes in various sizes.

After they'd left, Jenny stared in dismay at the confusion in her bedroom, wondering where to start. Shaking her head, she decided to completely ignore the mess and go for a swim. There would be time later to put everything away, and she'd been aching to try out the huge kidney-shaped pool since the moment she'd spotted it this morning.

She rooted among the clothes until she found a white one-piece bathing suit and the matching thigh-length beachrobe. She put them on quickly, slipped on a pair of sandals, and with one last guilty glance at the disaster in the bedroom, fled the apartment.

The enormous pool was lovely. Colorful umbrella tables and aqua and cream vinyl lounge chairs dotted the scene. Although the latter were crowded with sun worshipers, the pool itself was almost empty.

She took off her robe, draped it on an aqua lounge chair, slipped off her sandals, then ran eagerly to the iron ladder for the high dive. She supposed it was natural that swimming was her favorite sport after her years on Santa Flores. At Madame Junot's she'd perfected her strokes and won several diving medals.

She paused to catch her breath for a moment at

the top of the ladder before moving to the end of the diving board. She loved this moment just before the dive, when all her muscles tautened in anticipation and she went breathless with a combination of exhilaration and apprehension. She assumed position, unaware of the graceful, exotic picture she made against the skyline, with her shining black hair flowing almost to her waist and her arms outstretched like some ancient priestess praying to her gods.

She launched herself in a perfect swan dive, straightening to enter the water with the cleanness of an arrow.

It was glorious!

When she surfaced, she was surprised to hear a flurry of applause from the onlookers lolling around the pool. She did two laps, then climbed up the ladder at the side and padded around to her lounge chair. After settling herself comfortably on the recliner she pulled her hair over one shoulder. She was wringing the excess moisture out of it vigorously when a fluffy white towel with the hotel name embossed on it was tossed casually into her lap.

"Was that all for me? If it was, you succeeded. I'm quite impressed."

The young man standing before her was so blatantly male that Jenny stared. A little under six foot, he had a tanned muscular body shamelessly flaunted by black bikini trunks that were almost indecent. His hair was as black as a raven's wing, as were the dark eyes and almost girlishly long lashes. His sensual lips were parted in an intimate smile that revealed dazzling white teeth.

"I beg your pardon?" she said, thoroughly bewildered.

He squatted beside her and picked up the towel. "It worked. You won the jackpot." He ran the towel with outrageous intimacy over the hair that was lying over one shoulder. "Lord, that's lovely!"

"I don't know what you're talking about," she said icily, grabbing the towel. "But I wish you'd go away."

A frown creased his forehead. "Look, the game's over. You've won all the marbles. Drop the act."

"You're totally insane!"

Annoyance was building in that dark, handsome face. "Look, I don't have time for the second chorus." His hand fell with casual intimacy on her bare thigh.

Jenny jumped to her feet as if she'd been scalded. She backed away from him until she reached the edge of the pool, wondering if she'd have to dive in to escape this idiot.

He got slowly to his feet and strolled toward her. "You forgot something," he drawled, then put a hotel key in her hand and closed her fingers around it. "I'll meet you upstairs in ten minutes," he whispered.

She'd had enough of this sex-starved maniac. He had not only spoiled her swim, but he'd actually insulted her! Jenny could feel rage surge through her as her hand clenched around the key.

She spoke through her teeth. "You are the most obnoxious, the most conceited . . ." Her eyelids closed for a moment while she drew a shaky breath and fought for control. She opened them again and her silver eyes were blazing. She spat out furiously. "There isn't a convenient lake that I can tell you to jump into, so this will have to do!"

With a swift movement that caught him off guard, she placed both hands on his chest and pushed. His arms and legs flailed wildly as he fell backwards into the pool with a tremendous splash. With all her force she threw the key after him and stalked furiously away. She was still shaking with anger as she crossed to the recliner and picked up her robe. Slipping into it with jerky motions and then stepping into her sandals, she turned and walked swiftly toward the cabanas.

"Wait, damn it!" A wet hand grasped her arm and she turned to face the dripping form of her antagonist. His suave demeanor had vanished. Sopping wet hair was plastered to his forehead and his chest was heaving from the effort he'd expended as he ran to catch up with her. "I'm sorry! It was all a mistake! For heaven's sake, will you listen to me?"

She regarded him stonily. He did look funny, rather like a shivering puppy after a bath, she thought, her irritation ebbing fractionally.

"Please, will you just sit down and let me explain? I promise I won't come on to you like that again."

She studied him for a long moment before deciding to accede to his request. After all, he'd suffered more from the exchange than she. She followed him silently to a poolside table shaded by a gaily striped umbrella, and sat down stiffly on a white vinyl chair.

He collapsed into the chair opposite her with a profound sigh of relief, his breath still short. "I must be out of shape," he said, leaning back. "Look, it's all very simple. I'm Rex Brody."

She looked blankly at him.

"Rex Brody," he repeated, as if she couldn't have heard him.

"Jenny Cashman," she returned politely, wondering if she'd made a mistake in giving in to his request. The man was still behaving most peculiarly.

His face was a picture of amazement. "You don't know who I am?" he asked slowly. "I'm the headline singer at the Pagan Room."

"You're an entertainer?" she asked courteously.

"I'm a star," he corrected with a touch of indignation.

"Well, that's very nice, Mr. Brody. Now, if you'll excuse me . . ." She pushed back her chair.

He caught her arm again, stopping her from rising. He gazed intently into her indifferent face. "You don't care," he said, obviously thunderstruck. "It doesn't matter a damn to you. You'd have pushed me into the pool anyway!"

She looked down at his hand grasping her arm. "You're quite right, Mr. Brody," she said sweetly. "And if you don't remove your hand, it's entirely possible that I may do it again."

He jerked his hand away swiftly, raising it in surrender. "Just let me explain," he said softly. "Look, you may not have heard of me, but practically everyone else in the country has. I'm the hottest property in America right now." His words were matter of fact. "I've had one hit after another for the past three years, and I guess I've gotten used to women chasing me." He shrugged. "They like the glitter of the limelight, I suppose. I've had girls sneak into my hotel room, throw themselves in front of my car. They even toss me their room keys at the end of a performance."

Her eyes widened in shock.

He went on quickly. "When you made that spectacular dive, I thought you were just another groupie trying to get my attention." His dark eyes were sincere. "I know I behaved like a complete bastard. Will you forgive me?" His expression was boyishly appealing, and Jenny smiled reluctantly. He was actually quite likeable, now that he'd dropped that air of cynical arrogance.

"I suppose I should be flattered," she said doubtfully.

"Yep," he said, grinning. "I don't usually give my hotel keys to my fans. You really knocked me for a loop."

"In more ways than one," Jenny said, her eyes dancing as she remembered the ludicrous sight of Rex Brody falling backward into the pool.

He nodded ruefully. "You might say you made quite a splash with me."

She groaned. "That's terrible."

He grinned without shame. "Sorry, I couldn't resist it."

"My guardian is taking me to the Pagan Room tonight for dinner," she said. "Will you be performing?"

He nodded. "I'm booked for two weeks here before I start a cross country concert tour."

"You must be very good to be so well known at your age."

"I'm fantastic," he said simply.

She broke into helpless laughter that was impossible to suppress. He had the uncomplicated egotism of a child.

He looked momentarily disconcerted by her amusement, then grinned sheepishly. "I guess I've been reading too many of my own press clippings. I'd be lying if I didn't admit to being damn good though."

"I'm sure you are," she said, smiling.

"You'll see." He paused, then added, "Will you dance with me after the show?"

She studied him thoughtfully, deciding she liked the man beneath the facade. "That would be nice," she said.

He leaned back with a sigh of relief. "Good! I thought I'd blown it."

"I don't think you'd have found it difficult to find a replacement." Her gaze circled the pool area, noticing several ravishingly beautiful women in bikinis who were gazing at the singer with unabashed invitation in their eyes.

He shook his head mournfully. "Vegas is filled with Amazons. It seems to be some unwritten law that showgirls have to be at least six feet tall." He grimaced comically. "When I dance with a woman I detest getting a crick in my neck."

"So that's why you made me an exception," she teased. "I could have been a complete witch as long as I was tiny enough to look up at you admiringly."

He watched with fascination the play of emotions on her mobile face. "Not true," he said quietly, "I liked the look of you from the moment I saw you. You're not a razzle-dazzle bird, Jenny Cashman, but when a man looks at you, he wants to keep on looking."

She felt color rush to her cheeks, and her eyes dropped.

"You're blushing," he exclaimed delightedly. "I didn't think a girl existed who could still blush. It went out of style about the same time as virginity."

The blush increased to a betraying scarlet. She looked up in time to catch an expression of amazement on Brody's face. He gave a low whistle. "I'll be damned. That, too? I don't think I've ever met one."

"I'd rather not discuss it," she said icily, struggling to regain her dignity. This encounter was becoming increasingly bizarre.

"Okay," he said soothingly, his face amused. Then he muttered again, "I'll be damned!"

Jenny rose to her feet, anxious to escape. "I'll see you this evening, Mr. Brody," she said hurriedly.

"Rex," he corrected, standing also. "I think we've gone quite a few steps beyond formality, don't you, Jenny?"

She nodded, smiling wryly. "I think we have, Rex." With a wave of her hand, she walked away. Rex's eyes followed her until she disappeared into the hotel.

Jenny spent the rest of the afternoon putting away her morning purchases and tidying up her room. Then she showered, blew her hair dry, and sat down in front of the mirror for an hour's experimentation with the makeup kit.

When she'd put on the misty gray gown, she was amazed at the unfamiliar image in the mirror. It wasn't the sophisticated beauty she'd always admired, but she did radiate a romantic lushness that was very attractive. She sprayed herself lightly with Shalimar and slipped on the silver low-heeled sandals that she'd decided would be the most practical for dancing.

As she crossed the busy lobby on the way to the nightclub, she was pleasantly aware that she was receiving some very flattering glances. The pleasure ended abruptly when she caught sight of Steve waiting for her in the foyer. He wasn't alone.

The tall blond woman talking to him was incredibly attractive. Her voluptuous curves were daringly revealed in a strapless gown of emerald green lamé that echoed the exact shade of her eyes. Broad slavic cheekbones and full pouting lips lent a certain sexiness to her features, which would otherwise have been classical. Jenny sighed ruefully. So much for her new adult image. Steve had always chosen women who resembled fertility goddesses, and next to this one she probably appeared sexless.

Steve looked up idly and saw her. For a moment there was a curiously intent look on his face that was strangely predatory. Then it was gone, replaced immediately by tolerant amusement.

"Very nice," he commented as she joined them. "You've been busy." He turned to the blonde. "Cynthia, I'd like you to meet my ward, Jenny Cashman. Jenny, this is Cynthia Durand, a very talented singer in the Hut Lounge."

Cynthia Durand gave a cool little smile that didn't quite reach her eyes. "Steve tells me you're on holiday from school," she said smoothly. "I hope you won't find yourself bored. Las Vegas is really not a town for young people."

Thereby relegating me deftly to the nursery, Jenny thought wryly. "I'll try to keep myself amused," she returned politely. She'd learned long ago to ignore both the bitchiness and the saccharine sweetness of Steve's women. It hurt too much to let them get through her wall of reserve.

They were shown to a choice ringside table and served dinner by an eager-to-please young waiter who hovered constantly. The meal was impressive, but Jenny considered Mike's cooking better. Cynthia Durand dominated the conversation during the meal, speaking intimately to Steve for the most part. She occasionally threw Jenny a condescending comment like a bone to a dog, and Jenny was carefully polite. But she soon began to wish that she hadn't come. She doubted that Steve or his beautiful companion would miss her if she disappeared from the face of the earth.

Then she looked up from her dinner to find Steve's eyes fixed on her with an absorbed, impenetrable gaze. For a moment the electric blue eyes glowed with the same intimate, predatory look as when he'd first seen her in the foyer. Her breath caught in her throat as she returned the look helplessly, feeling that she was captured in a web of honey-sweet sensation. Then Cynthia distracted Steve's attention, placing one white hand on his arm and speaking softly to him. Jenny looked back down at her plate without really seeing it. She felt as shaken by that look as if he'd reached out and caressed her.

The cabaret show began directly after dinner, and it proved to be very good. First, there was the Follies Extravaganza, wherein an impossible number of incredibly beautiful girls paraded around in elaborate costumes that concealed practically nothing. She noticed with amusement that Rex was right. They were all quite tall, and also wore at least three-inch heels.

When the singer was announced, Jenny sat up with interest. Dressed in tight black velvet pants and a loose, long-sleeved silk shirt and black suede boots, Rex looked like a romantic pirate. Then he started to sing and she knew he was right—he *was* utterly fantastic. He hadn't been boasting at the pool this afternoon.

Rex was all over the stage at first, singing rock with a rhythmic frenzy that was electrifying. Then he switched to folk ballads, sitting on a plain wooden stool and crooning the simple words with heart-breaking poignancy. He manipulated his audience's emotions as skillfully as he did the strings of his guitar.

He received a standing ovation at the end of the show. As he stood with one hand raised in acknowledgement, his chest heaving, his face glowed with exhilaration. Jenny joined in the applause with such heartfelt enthusiasm that Cynthia Durand bestowed a vastly superior smile on her as Rex left the stage.

"You enjoyed it," she drawled. "I suppose he does seem quite good to those not in the business."

Steve arched an eyebrow. "He evidently appeals to practically everyone. I had to pay a small fortune to get him for this engagement."

"He's wonderful," Jenny enthused.

"I told you I was fantastic." Rex Brody spoke behind her. He'd hastily donned a velvet dinner jacket and changed his boots for polished black shoes, she noted, and his face was still aglow with exhilaration.

"You were super," Jenny said.

"Ah, respect at last!" he joked, then turned to Steve. "How do you do, Mr. Jason. I didn't realize you would be here this evening."

"You were very good, Brody," Steve said coolly. There was an intent gleam to his blue eyes. "I see you've met my ward. Do you know Miss Durand?"

Rex acknowledged the introduction with a polite nod before turning back to Jenny. "Well, mermaid, are you going to dance with me?"

She rose with an eager smile, excused herself to Steve and Cynthia, and preceded Rex to the dance floor. The orchestra was playing a mellow, languorous melody and Jenny slipped wordlessly into his arms. For a few minutes they danced silently.

Then Rex looked down at her, his expression whimsical. "You didn't tell me your guardian was Steve Jason."

She looked up in surprise. "I didn't think it mattered."

"It doesn't," he said casually. "But it was quite a surprise to see Steve Jason in the role of guardian to a young and innocent girl. Kind of like setting a wolf to watch the sheep."

Jenny looked away, a flush staining her cheeks. "He doesn't think of me in that way," she said awkwardly, with a fleeting memory of that sudden intimate look they'd exchanged.

"Then you're the only dolly he doesn't look on as a potential mistress. He has quite a reputation, you know."

"That doesn't concern me," she insisted, wishing disconsolately that it didn't. "Steve has taken care of me since I was a little girl."

"Well, just watch out when he discovers you're all grown up," Rex warned softly. Then he shrugged, and with a quick, boyish smile said, "Enough of this talking about another man. Let's concentrate on me."

Dancing with Rex was thoroughly enjoyable. Madame Junot may not have been heavy on the practical arts, but social graces were a must. They danced everything from disco to the tango, and they were both glowing and breathless when Rex finally returned Jenny to the table at the end of the set. She noticed that Steve and Cynthia were still on the dance floor as Rex seated her with graceful panache.

"I enjoyed it, mermaid," he said, grinning. "I wish I could stick around, but I've got to get ready for the next show." He ran his hand caressingly over her dark, shining hair. "May I call you tomorrow?"

She smiled back at him. "Of course!" The lively friendliness of Rex Brody was very endearing.

With a wave of his hand, he was gone. Jenny's smile lingered as she watched him hurry across the dance floor, avoiding with deft precision both the dancers and the eager fans who would have halted his progress.

"If you're quite finished making an exhibition of yourself, we'll leave," Steve said icily.

Jenny looked up, startled. She hadn't noticed that Steve and Cynthia had returned to the table. Her eyes widened in shock at Steve's words. Surely he must be joking. But there was no humor in his taut face. His blue eyes were blazing and his mouth was a hard tight line.

Cynthia chimed in sweetly, "You mustn't be upset with her, Steve. After all, she is very young and Rex does have a reputation as something of a charmer."

"Stay out of this, Cynthia. It isn't your concern," he said bluntly. "We're leaving, Jenny."

She opened her mouth to protest, but he forestalled her. "We'll discuss it later." She rose and followed them to the foyer. She had never seen Steve like this. He'd been displeased with her on occasion in the past, but he'd never displayed such a frightening intensity.

"Go on up to the apartment," he told her curtly as they reached the elevators. "I'll be up as soon as I put Cynthia in a cab."

"But, Steve, I thought we were going on to my place," Cynthia protested.

"Not tonight." His tone allowed no argument and the blonde threw Jenny a glance of poisonous dislike.

"Get moving, Jenny," Steve added over his shoulder. She reluctantly turned and entered the elevator, the happiness of just minutes ago completely gone.

When she entered the apartment, she continued through to the living room, turning on the lights as she went. Unwilling to sit and wait like a naughty child, she walked over to the stereo and put on a record. She didn't even notice what it was until the mellow voice of Johnny Mathis wafted through the apartment.

"I would have thought you'd have had enough romance for one evening," Steve said harshly from the doorway. He crossed to the stereo and switched it off, then stared at her, his jaw clenched. "You're here only one day, and you're already involved with a man whose reputation with women is known throughout show business."

"We're just friends," Jenny faltered, wondering what she'd done wrong.

"Where did you meet him?"

"I met him this afternoon at the pool," she answered quietly.

He took out a cigarette and lit it slowly, his blue eyes menacing. "You let him pick you up like some love-starved groupie?"

"He didn't pick me up," she protested, flustered. "Well, I guess he did, but it wasn't what you're implying."

Steve loosened his tie and unbuttoned the top button of his shirt. He walked over to the burgundy velvet couch opposite the stereo where Jenny still stood. He sat down, stretching his arm casually along the back.

"Tell me how it was, Jenny," he invited softly, his lip curling. "You seem a bit confused. Tell me how that over-sexed Romeo, whose affairs have been a legend since he was nineteen, picked you up." The last words were a savage snarl.

"You don't want to hear," Jenny said, turning away. "You don't want to believe me." This inquisition was becoming incredibly painful.

"I watched you this evening, letting that young idiot handle you, caress you, touch your hair." He drew a ragged breath. "I couldn't believe you were the same child I knew on Santa Flores."

"I'm not the same child," she answered sadly, her eyes bright with unshed tears. "I'm almost twenty." She turned back to him, her head raised proudly. "And how could you expect me to be the same person I was before, Steve? You've kept me so protected and pampered that I sometimes don't even recognize myself. I find myself leaning instinctively on you when I should be relying on my own independence and initiative. That child on Santa Flores was lonely and miserable, but she was also strong." Her silver eyes were steady on his. "You robbed me of that strength, Steve. Now I have to find a way of getting it back."

He breathed deeply, his lips twisting in a bitter smile. "So now I'm the villain of the piece. If you remember, you were very grateful for that protection at one time."

She ran her hand distractedly through her hair. "Do you think I'm not now?" she asked huskily. "It's just that it was all too much." She shrugged helplessly. "If you want that little girl back, you've got to set her free. I did nothing to be ashamed of tonight. I danced, I laughed, I had a good time. What's wrong with that?"

"Do you think that's all Rex Brody wants with you?" Steve said caustically, his eyes narrowed. "Do you know what Rex Brody considers a good time?"

"Probably the same thing you do." She crossed her arms to still their trembling. "He told me practically the same thing about you."

"Indeed?" he drawled. "You discussed me with Brody?"

"Not really. He just mentioned you had a bad reputation with women." She looked at him steadily. "I've always known that."

"Have you, Jenny?" he asked silkily. "I thought I'd kept that particular knowledge from you. Not that it matters." He got up slowly, crushing his cigarette out in the ashtray on the coffee table. "Because you're all grown up now and ready to face the big, bad world." He walked toward her like a stalking panther about to spring. "Since you know what a womanizer I am, you should realize I know what I'm talking about when I say I know what Brody wants." He halted within inches of her, gazing down into her face. His own face was almost expressionless with the exception of the blazing blue of his eyes.

"I don't understand," she stammered. "Why are you acting like this?"

He reached out and touched her quivering lips with a gentle finger, lazily tracing their outline. "I'm showing you how an experienced man operates," he said mockingly. "It's what every young girl needs to complete her education." His mouth twisted bitterly. "I just didn't think you were ready for it yet." His hands cupped her head, tilting it up so that their lips were just a breath apart.

She forgot to breathe, lost in the intimacy of the moment, her gaze clinging to his with the desperation of a drowning victim. "Close your eyes, Jenny," he ordered softly and she obeyed wordlessly. He kissed the closed lids with gentle, butterfly kisses. His lips slid caressingly over her cheekbones to hover over her mouth. "Be a good pupil, Jenny," he murmured. "Open your mouth."

She was a good pupil. She yielded her mouth to him like a flower to the sun. His tongue invaded her with a shocking sensuality that caused her hands to clench involuntarily. She felt a breathless warmth and a strange tingling sensation in the pit of her stomach. He deepened the kiss expertly before leaving her lips to bury his face in her hair. "Hold me, Jenny," he said huskily. "Touch me."

Her hands reached out hesitantly, and when she felt the warmth of his flesh beneath the white dress shirt, she experienced an almost physical shock. No one had ever told her that palms and fingertips could be so erotically sensitive. She slid her arms over his shoulders and around his neck, playing with the short gold curls at the nape. He was kissing her again, hot erotic kisses that turned her weak and boneless, and she moaned deep in her throat.

"You like that, hmm," he said, biting the lobe of her ear. "So do I." He lifted her, molding her hips to his with a motion that revealed his bold arousal. Her eyes flew open and he smiled at her. "See how much I like it?" he whispered.

He shifted his hold, picking her up and carrying her swiftly to the couch. He cradled her there in his arms, burying his hands in her hair while his lips brushed sensually along the sensitive cord of her neck. His hand moved to her back, and she felt her gown loosen suddenly as he deftly freed the zipper. He moved leisurely as if he had all the time in the world, as indeed he did, for she couldn't have moved from his arms if she'd tried. He bared the shoulder that had been covered by the gown and slid the chiffon down to her waist. He gazed for a long moment at the full proud lift of her breasts, and she felt them ache for his touch. Then he did touch them, and she drew her breath in sharply in a half gasp, half cry. His hands filled themselves with her, his thumbs teasing the peaks until they hardened with desire.

She arched achingly into his hands, and he looked up, his blue eyes hot and his breathing ragged. "So responsive," he murmured huskily. "It's really too bad that this is just . . ."

He removed his hands reluctantly, then lifted her from his lap onto the couch. He rose swiftly, putting the length of the room between them in a few seconds. He leaned against the bar and lit another cigarette, inhaling deeply.

He looked back at her, still sitting on the couch, her face dazed and strangely sensuous. "Cover yourself," he said tonelessly. "The party's over."

She sat up quickly, her hands fumbling frantically at the top of her gown. Steve's passionate lovemaking and then this sudden cold withdrawal had ripped her emotions to shreds. Tears flowed down her face as she tried futilely to fasten the zipper of the gown.

"Stop crying, you're not hurt," Steve said roughly, coming back to her and dealing swiftly with the zipper. His hands seemed to linger on the satin of her back before he drew a deep breath and backed away. His blue eyes were totally expressionless as he turned her around to face him. "But you could have been." His fingers tightened on her shoulders. "You're an easy mark for a man with any experience."

Not for any man, she thought hopelessly. Only you, Steve Jason.

"I want you to promise you won't see Rex Brody again," he said grimly. "You should be able to understand now that you're no match for a man like him."

"You're very cruel," she said, her voice flat. "Was all this necessary?"

"I thought so. I want your promise."

She stood up and walked toward her room, moving slowly as if she were a very old woman.

"Jenny?"

She turned the knob and leaned against the door for a moment, then without looking at him, said wearily, "You're not going to get it, Steve." She opened the door and closed it softly behind her.

Steve gazed at the closed door for a long moment before he muttered a violent curse and strode swiftly to the bar and poured himself a double Scotch. His hand was shaking as he lifted the glass to his lips, he noticed grimly. He felt as if he were being torn apart by the white-hot fury of jealousy that was surging through him. He closed his eyes and drew a deep shuddering breath. God, how much more of this could he take? He'd felt like killing that damned good-looking kid when he'd watched Jenny smiling up at him.

Kid. Yes, that was what had really bothered him. Brody was so damned *young*, only a few years older than Jenny herself. Watching them he'd felt the aching gap of years that separated Jenny from his own generation. It had hurt damnably and he'd struck out like an animal in pain. And it had been Jenny that he'd hurt. His Jenny.

A jolt of agony rocked him and he drained the glass with one swallow. He started to refill it, then slowly set the decanter down and pushed the glass impatiently aside. No amount of liquid comfort could soothe this particular ache. He'd found that out in the two years since he'd discovered that something new had entered his relationship with Jenny. He didn't know at exactly what point he'd realized that he wanted her as he'd never wanted a woman before in his life, but it had come as no real surprise. It had seemed natural somehow that he should experience all the ranges of emotion in his love for Jenny. She'd been only seventeen then and he'd known she must be protected from him as as-siduously as he would protect her from any other danger. He'd sent her away and carefully cut him-self off from any physical contact with her.

And all for nothing. For here she was, more beautiful than he'd ever dreamed she'd become, yet still his own strong, loving Jenny. Despite her ap-prehensions, Jenny had never lost that strength he'd seen shining out of her that first day on Santa

Flores. She could be right about his wanting to smother her with the good things of life. Lord knows, he'd wanted to give her the whole damn world to make up for the lousy start in life that bastard, Cashman, had handed her. His indulgence may have dimmed that bright serene flame, but it could never quench it. Every now and then he would capture a glimpse of that other Jenny at the most unexpected times and it filled him with an odd fear. If she ever regained that silent, tranquil fortitude, would she still be his own Jenny? Perhaps he'd deliberately fostered that naivete and dependency in her because of his fear.

Oh God, he just didn't know any more. All he knew was that in the past two days he had felt a constant ache of frustration and desire whenever he was in the same room with her. How the hell could he take the next two weeks without breaking? His control had almost blown sky-high tonight at the first real test, and he'd ended by causing that look of bruised pain on Jenny's face that had made him feel sick to his stomach.

He would have to take it. There was no real alternative. It would only be for another two weeks and then he'd whisk her back to Europe where she'd be safe from young studs like Brody and the even greater danger from himself. Pray God his restraint would last that long.

FOUR

JENNY AWOKE LATE the next morning and deliberately took her time showering and dressing. She flinched at the thought of facing Steve this morning. She hadn't slept for a long time the night before, her mind replaying that painful encounter until she'd fallen asleep from sheer exhaustion. What she couldn't comprehend was the cruelty of Steve's actions. She had known he was a tough, unrelenting man in both business and personal dealings, but he'd always protected her from that side of his nature. All that had ended when she'd defied him last night. He had turned on her the same implacable, ruthless force he displayed to everyone else, and she was suddenly a little afraid of him.

When she entered the breakfast room, Steve was still there, sitting with a cup of coffee in front of him and casually looking over a document he held. He had obviously been waiting for her to put in an appearance.

She murmured a subdued "Good morning" before slipping quietly into her place.

Steve's keen gaze raked her face, noting the dark circles beneath her eyes, but he made no comment.

Mike came in carrying a coffee pot. He refilled Steve's cup, then came around the table to fill Jenny's. "How about some pancakes this morning, chicken?" he asked.

"I just want some toast and orange juice, please, Mike," she said quietly.

Mike gave a snort of disgust as he disappeared back into the kitchen and returned with the toast. He poured her orange juice with definite signs of disapproval. Jenny watched with a faint glimmer of a smile as he stalked back into the kitchen.

"Mike at least thinks you're grown up," Steve

said dryly. "Six years ago he would have made you eat those pancakes."

"I know," she said, grateful for the small familiar incident that had fractionally lessened the tension between them.

"I waited for you because I want to talk to you," he said slowly, his gaze intent on her face.

"I'd rather not."

"We're going to talk just the same. I'm not going to let you brood about this and blow it up out of all proportion."

She sat silent.

"I was rough on you last night," he admitted coolly. "I lost my temper."

"You seemed in perfect control," she replied.

"Well, I wasn't." His mouth twisted wryly. "I don't apologize for my actions. People accept me for what I am, or not at all."

She smiled involuntarily at his sheer arrogance. Steve Jason would not apologize, but this came pretty close.

His tone was level as he continued. "What I really wanted to say is, despite what Brody may have told you about my reputation, you don't have to worry about what happened last night repeating itself." He smiled grimly. "Even if you weren't my ward, I don't make a habit of seducing virgins."

She looked down at her plate in sick despair. No, Steve would never be interested in inexperienced schoolgirls when he had his pick of more sophisticated women. She heard his chair being pushed back, and looked up to see him gathering up his papers.

"It won't be easy, but we can salvage our relationship, Jenny," he said crisply. "You've got to be willing to work at it, though." He paused. "I'll see you tonight."

She nodded.

When he'd gone, she sat for a moment thinking of what he'd said. There was no doubt in her mind that she wanted to save her relationship with Steve. He had been too much to her for too long. They were bound by ties and memories that would be agonizingly hard to discard.

But, good Lord, how was she ever going to forget last night? Now that she'd been made aware of the addictive delight of physical arousal by Steve, she knew she would crave that wizardry every time she was in his presence. Well, she would just have to get over that aching need for him. He had given her no choice, and life without Steve Jason was unthinkable.

Mike stuck his head out of the kitchen door. "Phone call for you, Jenny. There's an extension in the hall."

It was Rex on the line. "I hope you know what you've done to me, mermaid," he complained. "I am now occupying a two by four room over the kitchen. I've only slept in snatches all night."

"How is that my fault?" she asked, surprised.

"You threw my key in the pool."

"Which you richly deserved," she said tartly. "And the last I heard, the reception desk does have more than one key."

"They have keys, I have a key, and practically every girl in the follies has a key," he growled.

"What on earth are you talking about?" she asked, trying to unravel clarity from chaos.

"Some smart little cookie in the chorus saw you throw my key into the pool. She retrieved it, made about a dozen copies, and then sold them for a tidy little profit to the other girls in the show."

By the time he'd finished speaking, Jenny was leaning against the wall holding her sides, dissolved in laughter. "I think I get the picture," she gasped when she could speak again.

"Oh no, you don't. It wouldn't have been so bad if all they'd wanted was my virile young body, but I had a parade of Amazons through my room at 4 a.m. wanting to *audition* for me, for Pete's sake!"

Hearing her go off again in a peal of laughter, he said sourly, "I'm glad you're finding it so amusing. To top it off, the hotel is jammed with convention-eers and they had to stick me in this hole-in-the-wall room until hotel maintenance gets around to changing the locks on my suite."

"I'm truly sorry," she choked out, and then went off in gales of laughter again.

"I can tell," he said dryly. "Well, I'll chalk it up to experience, but you owe me one, Jenny."

"Granted," she said, wiping her eyes and regaining some semblance of composure.

"I'm glad you agree, because I'm collecting this afternoon. An old buddy of mine is having a barbe-cue at his ranch today. I want you to go with me."

She hesitated for only a moment. After all, she

hadn't agreed to Steve's arbitrary demands last night. Though discretion cautioned her to avoid Rex, she certainly needed something to revive her spirits and Rex Brody was a definite pick-me-up. She agreed cheerfully and arranged to meet him in the lobby in an hour.

A short time later they were speeding down the highway in Rex's rented Ferrari. Rex was indeed cheerful company. Jenny soon discovered he had a cynical dryness mixed with an irrepressible boyishness that was very likeable. His droll stories about his experiences on the road made the miles fly by, and they were soon turning off the main highway onto an access road.

The desert terrain was parched and barren and Jenny couldn't imagine it supporting life. When she made a comment on this to Rex he nodded. "You're right, it's not a working ranch. Danny Smith is a musician. He's one of the entertainers who work the Las Vegas clubs the year round. He calls it a ranch, but Danny wouldn't know a cow from a bull."

The ranch house they were approaching was a low, rambling adobe structure that glared white in the strong afternoon sun, its red tile roof giving it a vaguely Spanish flavor. The courtyard was filled with cars of every description, but Rex managed to find a parking place. When they rang the bell, the front door was thrown open and they were greeted by a loud blast of rock music.

"Rex, old buddy, it's about time you decided to come to one of my parties. We thought you'd forgotten your old pals."

Jenny stared in amused amazement at the man who had opened the door and stood grinning at them. He was tall, almost skeleton thin, with blazing red hair worn almost to his shoulders. He was dressed all in white—form fitting white suede pants, a white silk shirt, even soft white leather boots. He wore three glittering gold necklaces wrapped around his neck and there were several gold rings on the hand holding his drink.

"Jenny, I'd like you to meet Danny Smith. He's a bit insane, but one of the best drummers in the business. This is Jenny Cashman," Rex said.

"I am the best," Danny Smith corrected cockily.

Return to Santa Flores

"You haven't heard me lately." His gaze was running leisurely over Jenny's body in rude appraisal. He lifted his glass mockingly. "Welcome, Jenny Cashman. It's always nice to see a new face." His eyes were lingering with insulting intimacy on the pert thrust of her breasts in the aqua blouse.

Color flooded Jenny's face, and her temper rose to match. "I didn't think you'd noticed I had one," she said tartly.

Rex gave a snort of laughter and Danny Smith's gaze flew up to her indignant face with stunned surprise, his mouth agape.

"I forgot to tell you, Jenny isn't one of your usual birds," Rex said with malicious enjoyment at Smith's consternation.

The drummer recovered quickly, but his smile was a trifle thin. He obviously didn't like having his blasé image shattered. "Then you'd better take care of her," he replied with forced lightness. "If you remember, we're not exactly enthralled with puritans in our crowd."

"I intend to," Rex said.

Smith waved his hand. "Get yourself a drink and

enjoy. I'll pass the word that you're back in the fold." He vanished into the crowd.

Rex turned to Jenny with a rueful smile. "Sorry about that. Danny's not a bad guy. He's just a bit spoiled by the groupies who hang around the rock scene. You gave him quite a jolt."

He grabbed two glasses from a passing waiter's tray and handed her one. Taking her elbow he maneuvered their way through the crowd to a comparatively clear corner of the room. There was a terrible crush of people in the living room, and they were spilling out into the patio area. The music was deafening and the air heavy with smoke and perfume. Jenny could see Rex's mouth move but she shook her head helplessly, pointing to her ear to indicate that it was impossible to hear. He nodded and taking her arm again, spirited her through the crowd outside to the patio-pool area. That, too, was crowded, but at least they could hear.

"Some barbecue," she commented dryly.

"I'd forgotten what Danny's parties were like," Rex said, taking a swallow of his drink. "This is a pretty fast crowd. I used to run with them when I first hit it big. Then I realized that the booze and the coke were messing up my head, and I dropped out." His lips twisted. "It's a strange, freaky scene, but I thought you might find it interesting."

"It's certainly that," she agreed, staring in fascination at a woman whose face was painted dead white like a mime, a sunburst of black lines encircling her eyes.

Rex's face was sober as he said hesitantly, "Stay close to me, okay? Sometimes this gang goes a little too far."

"Why, Jenny, whatever are you doing here?" Cynthia Durand's voice was acid sweet.

Startled, Jenny looked up. The tall blonde was strikingly lovely; tight black satin pants and a gold blouse showed off her stunning figure.

"How do you do, Miss Durand," Jenny said politely. "This is a coincidence."

"Oh, everyone who's anyone eventually shows up at one of Danny's parties." Cynthia smiled archly. "Don't you find that true, Mr. Brody?"

Rex shrugged casually. "Danny usually manages to make things interesting."

Cynthia's laugh was brittle. "That's an understatement, but his choice of entertainment isn't exactly given a G rating." Her green eyes gleamed. "I'm amazed that Steve permitted you to come, Jenny. He does know you're here, doesn't he?"

"Does he know *you're* here, Miss Durand?" Jenny riposted.

"Oh, Steve and I have an open relationship." Cynthia waved a hand carelessly. "No strings on either side."

"You needn't worry about Jenny, Miss Durand," Rex interposed. "I intend to take good care of her."

"I'm sure that Steve would be simply thrilled to know that," Cynthia said with saccharine sweetness. "Well, I suppose you know what you're doing." She turned and swayed sinuously across the patio toward the house.

Rex made a face. "Charming lady."

Jenny nodded. "But she's very lovely," she said wistfully.

Rex shrugged indifferently and quickly changed the subject. For the next hour or so Jenny had a reasonably good time, though she found it difficult to relax with these rather bizarre people. She did find that they had a certain fascination. Rex supplied an anecdote for practically everyone to whom

she was introduced. They ate a little of the some-
what ordinary buffet that was spread on a long
table on the patio, talked desultorily, and did quite
a bit of people watching. They were just thinking
of leaving the party and making their way back to
the hotel when Danny Smith pushed his way
through the crowd toward them.

"So this is where you disappeared to. I've been
trying to find you, man," Smith said. He was sway-
ing slightly, his eyes a little unfocused. "Chico
Rivera is here."

"Chico, here? I thought he was still playing that
club on Bourbon Street," Rex exclaimed, his eyes
lighting up.

Smith shook his head. "He's back in Vegas for a
four-week gig at the Solitaire. He's sitting in with
the boys for a few numbers. Why don't you go say
hello?"

Rex nodded eagerly. "I will." He turned to Jenny.
"Chico and I started out together in the same band.
He's been in New Orleans for the past few years.
Come along, I'll introduce you."

Jenny shook her head, smiling. She had no wish
to go back into the crush inside. "I'll wait for you

here," she promised. "You'll want to talk over old times."

He hesitated briefly, then said, "Okay. I'll be back in a few minutes." He vanished into the crowd.

Danny Smith lingered behind. "He won't, you know," he said softly. "Chico will talk him into sitting in, and he'll forget the time. He always does. You'll be lucky if he remembers you in an hour."

Jenny shrugged uneasily. She had no desire to be alone among these people for any length of time. "Well, then I'll join him," she said lightly.

"And spoil his fun?" Smith shook his head. "You wouldn't want to do that. I've got a better idea."

She eyed him cautiously. "A better idea?"

"You don't feel comfortable with our little group, do you?" he asked silkily. "When I bought this place, I remodeled the entire stable area. Would you like to walk down and take a look at it?"

The idea was appealing. She'd had enough of this artificial atmosphere. She began to think she'd misjudged Danny Smith. He was being surprisingly understanding.

"I'd like that." She nodded.

"I thought you would. You impressed me as being the wholesome outdoor type."

He took her arm and led her across the patio and through a Spanish archway that led to the rear of the hacienda. It was mercifully quiet as they made their way toward a long white building some distance from the main ranch house.

"Do you have many horses, Mr. Smith?" Jenny asked curiously. Rex had mentioned that this wasn't a working ranch, and Danny Smith certainly didn't give the impression of being an equestrian.

He laughed shrilly, his voice strange. "Well, I've been known to use 'horse' occasionally."

She stared at him in bewilderment, suddenly disliking the wild look in his eyes.

She stopped abruptly. "Perhaps this isn't such a good idea. Rex may be looking for me. I think I'll go back to the patio."

Smith's sinewy hand fastened on her wrist. "Oh no, Jenny, not till you've visited the stable," he drawled. "I've been looking forward to having you there ever since you smarted off to me in front of Rex."

She struggled to pull her wrist from his hold, but he was surprisingly strong.

"I don't like bright little girls who think they're better than me." Smith's smile had an ugly twist to it. "I have a little special treatment in mind for you." He gave a high giggle. "Maybe a little angel dust for Rex's little angel."

Jenny felt her heartbeat increase and a panicky fear rise in her. She started to fight him in earnest as he forced her toward the stable doors.

"Let her go, Smith." The words were as steely and menacing as a drawn stiletto.

They both looked up. Steve Jason was standing quite still, but every muscle of his body was coiled with tension. He was wearing a dark business suit and looked tough and competent and blessedly safe. Jenny gave a relieved sigh. Everything would be all right now.

"This is none of your business, Jason," Smith snarled. "Since when have you started to play Sir Galahad?"

Steve moved with lightning swiftness. In three quick movements, it was all over. One stride to bring him within striking distance, a numbing karate chop to Smith's forearm that caused him to release Jenny's wrist, and a sudden jerk that brought her within the circle of his arm. Jenny buried her face in his shoulder, shaking with both fear and relief.

Smith was cursing steadily, his hand cradling his useless arm, his face red with fury. "You may have broken my arm, damn you!" he cried shrilly, his eyes wild. "And for what? She's just a little 'friend' of Brody's!"

Jenny felt the arm tighten around her like a steel band.

"You're wrong, Smith," Steve's voice was soft and deadly. "She belongs to me, and if I ever catch you within touching distance of her again, I'll break more than your arm."

There was a flicker of fear in Smith's face as he licked his lips nervously. "How was I to know that she was your property?" he whined. "She came with Rex. You know I wouldn't try anything with one of your women, Mr. Jason."

There was a contemptuous curl to Steve's lips as he took in the sudden shift in Smith's attitude. "You'd better not make that mistake again, Danny," he said, his eyes narrowed. "No matter who Jenny's with when she goes out, she always comes home to me."

He turned and half led, half carried Jenny across the stable yard and around the hacienda to the front courtyard where his Mercedes was parked. She followed meekly, wanting only to put as much distance as possible between herself and Danny Smith. It was only after Steve had seated her in the car and slid behind the steering wheel that she remembered Rex.

"Wait." She put a restraining hand on Steve's arm as he started the engine. "I've got to tell Rex we're leaving."

He looked down at her, his face hard, his blue eyes glittering with the same menace that had shaken Smith. "I'm going to say this only once, Jenny," he said softly. "You're never going to see Brody again."

Her eyes dropped before the barely controlled rage in his. They were on the highway, fast approaching Las Vegas before she spoke again. "It wasn't Rex's fault. He didn't have anything to do with it," she said stubbornly.

His hand tightened on the steering wheel. "He took you there," he said. "Are you so crazy about him that you can't see that he belongs to that crowd? He's just like them."

"Not any more," she insisted. "He hasn't seen any of them for years."

"He knew what kind of place he was taking you to. Even he should know you don't take a school kid to one of Danny Smith's parties. They're notorious in Las Vegas."

"Miss Durand was there," she countered, then looked up in startled realization. "She called you, didn't she? She told you where I was."

"It was fortunate that she did," he said grimly. "I didn't get there a minute too soon. I don't think you'd have enjoyed Danny Smith's 'stable.'"

She shivered uncontrollably. "I thought he was going to show me his horses."

"Only an innocent like you would fall for a line like that." The look he gave her was scathing. "The stable is where Smith holds his wilder parties. Shall I tell you what you could expect there?"

"No, I think I can imagine," she said quickly, wanting only to forget that moment of terror.

Steve pulled into the car park at the Santa Flores, then silently escorted her to the elevator and up to the apartment. He strode over to the bar, poured himself a whiskey and drank half of it down before turning to where she was patiently waiting. "All right," he demanded, "let's have it. Why did you go out with Brody? I thought I'd made it clear that you weren't to see him again."

"I like him," she said simply. "I'm not a child who obeys blindly any more, Steve. I've got to make my own decisions and my own mistakes."

His hand tightened on the glass. "You almost made a hell of a mistake today. And while I'm in charge of you, I'm going to do my damndest to see that you don't make any more."

"You can't live my life for me. I've got to learn through experience like everyone else."

He tossed down the rest of his drink. "Well, you're not going to gain experience in Danny Smith's 'stable,' or as Rex Brody's latest mistress."

The tears welled up unexpectedly, as Steve's anger together with the terror she'd experienced earlier suddenly became too much to bear. She stood looking at him helplessly while the tears rolled slowly down her cheeks.

"Hell!" Steve exclaimed. In four strides he was across the room and picking her up. He sat down in the burgundy easy chair and cradled her in his arms. She clung to him tightly, her head against the fine material of his jacket while convulsive shudders shook her.

"I was so afraid until you came," she whispered brokenly.

"Forget it. I did come. I'll always be there when you need me, Jenny." His arms were a warm tender shelter containing all the security in her world. His hand pressed her head to his chest while her tears dampened the linen crispness of his shirt. "God, please don't cry," he said thickly. "It rips me apart." He drew a deep breath, his hand automatically stroking the dark silkiness of her hair. "When you were a child, you never cried, no matter how hurt or frightened you were. Remember how terrified you were of storms? You'd turn pale as a ghost and flinch at every crash of thunder, yet you'd never say a word. It used to break my heart to watch you."

"I didn't realize that you knew," she said shakily, her voice muffled in his shirt front.

"I knew. I would have liked to have snatched you up and cuddled you like this, but you were so gallant, so dignified. I was afraid of crushing your bravery. So I pretended I didn't notice and just tried to distract you."

"You taught me to play poker," she murmured, remembering the patient hours he'd devoted to teaching her the rudiments of the game through those long stormy periods. In her frantic relief she'd never thought to question his sudden appearance when the thunder had rolled and the lightning had ripped through the tempest-darkened skies. He'd been a terribly busy man, even then, yet he must have left his business affairs any number of times to come and lend her the support of his presence. And she had never known. In how many other ways had Steve sheltered and cared for her that she'd never been aware of?

"Even after you'd gone off to school and were thousands of miles away, it would worry the hell out of me whenever a storm blew up." He shook his head. "My reason kept telling me that the sun was probably shining where you were, but I never could be logical about you, Jenny."

"Oh, Steve." Her throat ached and her arms tightened around him fiercely.

"There are all kinds of storms out there in the world, Jenny." His deep voice was mesmerizingly tender in her ear. "Let me shelter you from a few of them. Don't make me stand by again and watch you suffer. It hurts me too much."

Jenny felt an explosion of emotion so intense that it took her breath away and she closed her eyes, unable to speak for a moment. She knew that Steve had given her an incredibly precious gift in those simple words. It must have been agonizingly diffi-cult for a man of Steve's pride and strength to ex-pose his vulnerability like this. "I don't want to ever make you unhappy, Steve," she whispered throatily, burrowing her head deeper in his shoul-der. "I'm sorry I've been such trouble for you. I don't mean to be."

His husky laugh reverberated beneath her ear. "It's not often you're so docile. I'm tempted to take advantage of it to wring a few sensible commit-ments from you."

She sat up, pushing herself away, her eyes clear pools of sincerity. "I always want to do what you want me to, Steve," she said quietly.

His mouth twisted as his fingers traced the path of her tears down one cheek. "I know you do, Jenny." His voice was as gentle as his touch. "So why can't you let me take care of you? Why do you persist in hurting yourself by fighting me?"

The brilliant blue eyes were lit with a rare tenderness, and she was tempted to surrender to anything that he asked just to keep this precious happiness between them. "I want to say yes, now," she said honestly. "But tomorrow I know I'll feel the same as before."

"Listen, Jenny." Steve's expression was dead serious. "You mean something very special to me, and I can't let you take the risks that you did today. I nearly went crazy when I saw that bastard with his hands on you. I'm giving you fair warning—there isn't anything I wouldn't do to prevent that happening again."

He smiled then and pushed her gently off his lap, swatting her seat lightly. "Now, why don't you go lie down and rest, and let me get back to work?"

Jenny turned and walked toward her room.

"And Jenny!"

She turned inquiringly to meet his wry smile.

"Try to stay away from any major catastrophes until I get home for dinner."

FIVE

JENNY TRIED VERY hard in the next week to obey Steve's injunction to keep out of trouble. She read, sunbathed, talked to Mike, and waited patiently for Steve to come home in the evening.

Steve, too, appeared to be making special efforts to regain their old companionship. Instead of going out after dinner, he spent the evenings at home alone with her. They listened to music, talked for hours, and Steve began to teach her how to play backgammon. It was a curiously contented time, seemingly isolated from the tension that had surrounded their relationship since she'd first returned. It was as if Steve had turned back the clock, and that evening when he'd started to make love to her had never existed. In his eyes she was still the little sister she always had been to him. If there were moments when he brushed against her accidentally and she felt a sudden breathless shock, there was no sign on Steve's impassive face that he felt any similar emotion.

She hadn't heard from Rex Brody since that disastrous afternoon at Danny Smith's, though she suspected Steve had spoken to him and warned him off. But she didn't ask about it. The fragile understanding between them would not bear the strain of any conflict.

On Tuesday morning Jenny was called to the phone by Mike, not realizing that it was a summons that would bring about a myriad of changes in her life.

"Jenny, this is Carol Morris. I met you at the boutique in the lobby. Do you remember?"

"Yes, of course," Jenny answered. "Your family is here for the medical convention. Are you enjoying yourselves?"

"Well, my father is having a ball," Carol said

candidly. "But Scott and I are bored to tears. Why don't you have pity and let us take you to lunch?"

"I have a better idea. Why don't you both come up and have lunch with me," Jenny said warmly. "Our cook can provide a much better meal than any of the hotel restaurants."

"That sounds super!" Carol agreed without hesitation. Jenny suggested one o'clock and after chatting a few minutes, the other girl hung up.

Jenny went immediately into the kitchen to tell Mike that there would be three at lunch. He was as pleased as she'd thought he would be. Mike loved to show off for company, and there had been no opportunity since she'd returned. With a feeling of anticipation, she went directly from the kitchen to her room to change. It would be fun to have guests of her own, and she'd liked Carol Morris very much that day in the shop.

She slipped on a pair of carnation pink silk hostess pajamas that gave her a vaguely oriental air and put her hair in a knot on top of her head, leaving a few wisps to float seductively about her face. She made up her face carefully, and put on a pair of high-heeled sandals. The reflection in the mirror pleased her; she looked quite the mature, sophisticated hostess.

This opinion was echoed by the expression on Carol's face when Jenny opened the door to her ring. "Wow! You look great," she said, gazing enviously at the hostess pajamas. Carol herself was dressed in an obviously expensive yellow linen dress and was as glowingly attractive as Jenny remembered.

"Thank you," Jenny said, smiling. "So do you."

"Jenny, I'd like you to meet my brother, Scott," Carol said proudly, gesturing to the man standing beside her.

Scott Morris was everything Carol had said he was. He had the same glossy brown hair and sparkling brown eyes as his sister, but there the resemblance ended. Tall, broad shouldered, slim hipped, he looked every inch the football hero Carol had described. That he was aware of his good looks was obvious in the flashing, confident smile he bestowed on Jenny as he covered her small hand with his own in a lingering handshake.

"I'm happy to meet you, Scott," Jenny said politely. "Won't you both come in?" She led them to the living room and invited them to sit down.

Carol was looking around with wide eyes, taking in every detail of the luxurious decor. "What a beautiful room!" she exclaimed. "Is the rest of the apartment this gorgeous?"

"Thank you," Jenny said. She had grown so used to it she'd forgotten how impressive she'd found the apartment that first day. "Yes, it's all quite lovely. Steve had the same decorator who did the hotel in to do the apartment."

"Will he be joining us for lunch?" Carol asked eagerly, and her face dropped in disappointment when Jenny shook her head.

"Steve is rarely home at this time of day. He's addicted to conducting business over lunch," Jenny said, making a face.

"He must be a fool to leave someone as lovely as you alone." Scott spoke for the first time.

Jenny had been conscious that he'd been eyeing her with an extremely intimate stare since he'd entered the living room, but she'd chosen to ignore it. Now, she just shrugged. "It doesn't matter. We have the evenings."

"I'm sure you do," he said obliquely.

Mike called them to lunch then and Jenny led the way to the dining room. Mike's shrimp crepes were absolutely heavenly, followed by strawberry cheesecake and coffee. Both the Morrises were loud in their praise of the meal, and the talk over lunch was bright and casual. Jenny told them of her visit to Paris, and they described the Southern California way of life to her. Though Jenny didn't like Scott Morris nearly as much as his sister, he did put himself out to be agreeable over lunch and she found that he could be surprisingly charming.

They lingered over coffee a long time, and when Carol and Scott announced that they must go, Jenny felt a twinge of regret. It had been fun.

As she saw them to the door, Carol asked tentatively, "I don't suppose you'd like to go sightseeing with us tomorrow? Have you ever been to Hoover Dam?"

Jenny shook her head. "I've heard of it, of course. Is it near here?"

"Close enough," Scott said in a persuasive voice. "I've rented a car, and Carol and I thought we'd drive up and take the tour. On the way back we're going to take a detour and stop off at Caleb's Gulch."

"Caleb's Gulch?"

"It's an old ghost town that Scott discovered last summer when he and his fraternity brothers were racketing around the desert," Carol explained eagerly. "I've been trying to persuade him to take me there since he first told me about it."

"I'd like to go," Jenny decided. "Shall I meet you in the lobby?" They set a time for noon the next day and she closed the door behind them with a happy smile.

She was careful to tell Steve of her plans over dinner. She wanted no repeat of the incident of the Smith barbecue to destroy the contentment of their rapprochement.

"Scott and Carol Morris?" Steve frowned.

"Carol said they'd been introduced to you. Her father is the chairman of the medical convention."

Steve's face cleared and he nodded. "Sam Morris. They seem to be nice enough kids," he said indulgently. "And you'll enjoy the tour. Why don't you have Mike fix you a picnic lunch?"

Jenny's happiness at his agreement was mixed

with bittersweet wistfulness at his avuncular attitude. Would he never see her as an adult, ready to meet him on his own level?

No trace of sadness remained when she made her way to the lobby the next afternoon, picnic basket in hand. The sun was shining brightly and she was eagerly looking forward to the jaunt.

Scott Morris met her with a wide smile, taking the basket from her and grasping her arm possessively. He was dressed in casual khakis, a cream T-shirt, and tennis shoes, and looked tanned and cleancut. "You look good enough to eat," he said with a flashing smile. "And right on time, too. I like punctuality in my women."

Jenny was startled at the extravagant compliment. She was dressed in blue jeans and a tailored white blouse and sandals. Though adequate, her appearance certainly didn't warrant Scott's apparent enthusiasm.

"Carol's not down yet?" she asked as he shepherded her toward the car park.

"Carol's a bit under the weather," Scott said, grinning unsympathetically. "Nothing serious, just an upset stomach, but she wasn't up to the long drive."

"I'm sorry to hear that," Jenny said, frowning. "Perhaps we'd better postpone the trip until tomorrow."

Scott shook his head. "She'd feel terrible if she thought she'd spoiled your day. We'll go on, and plan to do something else with her tomorrow."

Jenny nodded doubtfully, but got into the dark blue sedan when he held the door open for her. She was very disappointed at Carol's defection. The day wouldn't be nearly as enjoyable without her perky enthusiasm.

The sun was almost down when they reached Caleb's Gulch. Long shadows cast eerie patterns on the sun-dappled streets and dark, blank windows stared sightlessly at them as Scott brought the car to a halt. Despite the air of desolation, Jenny found nothing frightening about the ghost town. Instead, it struck her as rather sad and pitiful, consisting of only two short streets lined with ramshackle wooden buildings, over half of which were either partially or totally collapsed. Here and there stood a building totally intact, obviously better built than the others. A breath of wind stirred, sending a tumbleweed scurrying across the wide street to come to rest against the broken remains of a hitching rail.

"Who was Caleb?" Jenny asked, thinking sadly of the people whose dreams had been born and died in those pathetic houses.

"Who knows?" Scott shrugged indifferently. "Most of these towns were named after the miner who made the first strike." He reached over to the cooler in the backseat and brought out another can of beer. Tearing off the tab, he drank thirstily. "Yep, old Caleb was probably the big man around here till the silver ran out."

Jenny watched a little apprehensively as Scott gulped down the beer in an amazingly short amount of time. He'd been drinking steadily since they'd stopped for lunch at the roadside picnic area after the tour of Hoover Dam, and she'd been distinctly uneasy about coming to this deserted ghost town with him. But her tentative arguments had met with surprising belligerence on his part, and he did seem in fairly good shape despite the amount of alcohol he'd consumed. Though his words were a little slurred and his jokes slightly more risqué, his driving ability hadn't seemed to be impaired, and he'd been perfectly charming to her before he'd started drinking. Perhaps everything would be all right after all.

"Let's get out and explore," Jenny said eagerly, reaching for the handle of the door.

Scott shook his head. "It's too damn hot," he said peevishly. "Who wants to wander around a bunch of crummy shacks?"

"Well, I think I'll just take a look around," she said firmly, getting out of the car. There was no way she was going to leave this fascinating place without a closer look. Actually she was relieved to be free of Scott's company for a bit. It was becoming a strain to hide her increasing nervousness of the man.

For the next twenty minutes she wandered happily in the dusty ruins. The saloon and the hotel were the only buildings that appeared to be in anything resembling their original condition. She explored the ground floor of each, but was afraid to climb the rickety stairs to the upper floors. She was about to embark on her investigation of the second street when she heard the raucous blowing of a horn. With a resigned sigh she turned and walked slowly back to the car.

When she climbed into the passenger seat, Scott grumbled impatiently. "It's about time."

"I'm sorry to have kept you waiting," she said politely, gritting her teeth over the necessity of being courteous. "We can leave now."

"I'm in no hurry," Scott said, leering unpleasantly. "I was just lonesome." His hand reached down to fondle her thigh.

She moved away hurriedly. "It's late." She tried to keep her voice steady. "It'll be getting dark by the time we get back to Las Vegas."

He slid closer to her, trapping her against the door. "So what? I'm beginning to enjoy myself for the first time today." He crushed his lips down on hers, holding her head still by tangling his hands in her hair. His lips were moist, his breath smelled of sour beer.

When he raised his head there was a self-satisfied smile on his face. "I've wanted to do that since I saw you yesterday," he said. "You looked so cute and sexy in that chinese thing."

"Let me go!" she said through her teeth, struggling furiously. "I can't stand you touching me."

"No way," he said smugly. "Relax, you'll love it. I'm as good as Steve Jason any day."

She tried to wriggle free but his weight prevented her from moving, and her movements only seemed to inflame him. His lips pressed against her own in another suffocating kiss. It disgusted her. She bit down on his lip as hard as she could.

He raised his head with a startled curse. "You little bitch."

"Let me go, Scott!"

"You're so high and mighty," he sneered, his hands in her hair jerking her head back painfully. "Who do you think you're fooling? All I'm asking is that you give me a little of what you give Jason every night."

"Steve is my guardian," she gasped, straining frantically to get away.

"My dumb little sister may believe that story, but she's the only one," he said, his smile ugly. "Steve Jason keeps a luscious little teenager in his apartment and lets her buy anything she wants. Who'd be stupid enough to believe that he's going to keep his hands off her?" He leered at her. "You must be good, honey. I hear Jason's never kept a live-in mistress before."

He removed one hand from her hair to fumble at the buttons on her blouse. When her desperate writhing frustrated his attempts to unbutton the garment, he impatiently grabbed the neck of it and pulled down brutally. The blouse gave way, buttons flying in all directions, and for one horrible moment she felt his hand on her breast.

Jenny screamed as loudly as she was capable, and at the same time butted his mouth with her head. For a brief moment his grasp loosened and she had the car door open and was out of the car in a flash. She ran. The sounds of his pursuit came swiftly— the opening of the car door, his muttered obscenities, the sound of his feet pounding on the hard-baked earth. Her heart was beating crazily as she looked frantically for a place to hide.

She ducked between two buildings, jumping over a pile of refuse, and dashed around the back. She could hear him behind her. Oh God, what if he was faster than she was? He was an athlete, wasn't he? Weren't quarterbacks supposed to be fast? She cast a look behind her. He hadn't reached the back of the building yet, thank God.

The hotel! There was a flight of back stairs leading to an overhanging balcony. She flew up the stairs, praying they would hold her slight weight. There was a gaping window at the head of the steps and she swung over the sill into the darkness.

The sun had set now, and she could make out nothing in the room. She stood pressed against the wall to the side of the window, her breath coming in gasps. She could hear him now, coming fast, bellowing her name in fury. Had he seen her run up the stairs? He hadn't. He passed on. She relaxed fractionally as his voice faded when he turned a corner and took the next street. She stayed there a long time, frozen into a cold panic. Scott came by twice more. If possible, the rage in his voice had increased, but he never tried the stairs.

About forty minutes passed since the last time Scott had come by and Jenny realized she heard nothing now. No, that wasn't true. She did hear something, but it wasn't outside. It was in the room with her.

She couldn't breathe, her heart was pounding so hard it was choking her. There was something obscenely horrible about standing here in the darkness, totally oblivious of her surroundings or what horrors they might contain. She heard it again. A soft, slithering sound.

She dove through the window and landed in a roll on the balcony that cracked ominously as she hit the rotten boards. She ran helter-skelter down the stairs, not caring if Scott Morris or the devil himself might be at the bottom of them. For the moment either seemed the lesser evil. She made it to the ground and clutched the rail, trying to catch her breath. Her hand pressed against her side to quiet the heart that was trying to jump out of her body. Her mind told her that what had been in that room was probably harmless to her. She shook her head. That slither had had a definite reptilian sound. She would have to find some other place to hide.

Jenny crept silently along the side of the hotel until she came to the open street. She cast a cautious glance to where Scott had parked the car, thinking he might have returned there to wait her out. What she saw caused her to stop abruptly. Then she moved dazedly to the center of the empty street. There was nothing there! He had taken the car and gone back to Las Vegas. She was alone in Caleb's Gulch.

For the first moment Jenny felt only a sense of outrage that Scott had dared to leave her alone in a deserted ghost town in the middle of nowhere. Then came an overpowering sense of relief that she was free from the menace that had stalked her. She gave a shaky laugh that echoed bell-like on the clear night air. What had she expected, for heaven's sake? She wouldn't have gotten in that car with Scott if her life had depended on it. She'd spent nearly two hours trying desperately to avoid him and now she was indignant that he'd finally given up and she was rid of him!

Her shoulders straightened and her chin lifted in determination. It wasn't as if the situation was a complete disaster. She was young and strong and could survive a night in the desert if she had to. Her lips curved in a wry smile as she remembered she'd told Steve she wanted to regain her former strength and independence. Well, she'd certainly landed herself in a situation that would demand an abundance of those qualities.

The thing to do was not to panic, but try to consider her options. There were only two, she thought ruefully. Start walking back to Las Vegas and run the risk of getting lost in the desert, or stay here in Caleb's Gulch and wait for rescue. There was no doubt in her mind that Steve would come eventually. He knew who had accompanied her on this trip today, and nothing or no one could withstand Steve when he wanted something bad enough. It was just a matter of time before he extracted the location of her whereabouts from Scott.

The decision made, there only remained for her to make herself as comfortable as possible until Steve arrived. She looked around the street appraisingly. There was a full moon, thank goodness. At least she wouldn't be blundering around in total darkness. One thing was sure, she thought with a shiver: She wasn't going to take shelter in any of the buildings. Nights in the desert could be surprisingly chilly, so she would need some source of warmth. She looked down at her torn blouse, noting that it was beyond repair. There wasn't a button left on it. She shrugged philosophically, then gathered the tails of the tattered blouse and tied them in a knot to get them out of the way.

In the next hour she busied herself gathering wood for a fire. There was certainly enough lying around; some of the shacks were one big trash heap. While collecting wood, she ran across a treasure trove, if several discarded tin cans could be so described. When she judged she had enough wood, she returned to the middle of the street where she had deposited her loads. She then gathered an armful of sage brush for kindling.

The problem of starting the fire was a different proposition. Everyone knew the principle of starting a fire by friction, but applying it was another matter entirely. After selecting two stones, she bent her efforts toward her desired goal with an enthusiasm that waned rapidly at the frustrating task. But at last she had the desired spark and she scrambled hurriedly to nurture it into a small blaze. Sitting back on her heels, Jenny gazed at the fire with all the triumph of a winning athlete at the Olympic games. She added a bit more wood to the fire, then looked around for her next project.

She chose a large can with a peaches label and scrubbed the interior with sand. She then carried it to the rusty pump at the watering trough in front of the hotel. She worked for some minutes pumping the handle vigorously. Nothing came out but a puff of dust and she sighed in discouragement. It was probably too much to hope that the well wouldn't be dry after all these years. She'd give it another ten minutes. In five, a narrow trickle emerged from the curved nozzle. She redoubled her efforts excitedly, and suddenly the water gushed out explosively. She hurriedly put the can beneath the flow and washed it thoroughly. Then filling it to the brim she returned to the fire.

Jenny put more wood on the blaze and settled herself beside it. She placed the can of water on a flat stone, and nudged it close enough to the flames to heat it without scorching the can. When it was warm, she lifted it gingerly and took a small drink. The acrid well-water together with the taste of tin was definitely bitter, but at least it was warm. As a cool breeze stirred, she drew closer to the fire and settled down to wait.

Jenny had no idea how much time had passed when she finally saw the pinpoints of headlights in the distance. It must have been several hours for she'd had to restock her supply of wood twice, and she was once again running low. She breathed a sigh of relief as the car ate up the miles between them like a hungry dragon with jewel-bright eyes. She must be more tired than she had thought to be so fanciful at a time like this, she mused. She rubbed her neck tiredly, then picked up her can to warm her hands on the metal.

She waited patiently as Steve's Mercedes covered the last hundred yards and then halted with a screech of brakes a short distance from where she sat by the fire. The car door slammed, and Steve tore around the car with angry strides.

He was dressed in black jeans and desert boots, his black sport shirt unbuttoned at the throat to reveal his strong bronze throat. He looked virile, tough, and dangerous. And angry, oh yes, very angry. His raking glance took in her diminutive form sitting crosslegged in front of the flames, can in hand, and a sardonic smile twisted his lips.

"You appear to have made yourself right at home," he said sarcastically. "A warm fire, a hot drink. I'm surprised you didn't make yourself some rattlesnake stew."

"I tried, but I couldn't catch one," Jenny said flippantly.

He reached her in one stride, dragging her to her feet and shaking her roughly. His mouth was tight, his blue eyes blazing. "I'm glad you're finding this so amusing." His voice was hoarse with fury. "I've been through hell thinking you were dead or raped or lost in this lousy desert, and you sit there and make jokes!"

Her eyes blazed back at him. "Would you prefer it if I wailed and beat my head on the ground?" she asked with equal fury. "I've had a rotten night and your attitude isn't guaranteed to make me feel any better! How the hell do you know that I *haven't* been raped?"

He went perfectly still, his eyes becoming

strangely blank. His hand touched her torn blouse jerkily, as if noticing it for the first time. "Were you?" he asked thickly. "Did that bastard rape you?"

She was so enraged that she was unaware of the coiled tension of his stance. "You come here roaring at me," she ranted on, "blaming me for something—"

"Jenny!" His voice cut through her tirade sharply. "Answer me, did he take you?"

"No!" she shouted at him. "But that doesn't—"

He made an inarticulate sound and she was crushed against his chest, his heartbeat a rapid pounding beneath her ear. "Damn you!" he said raggedly. Then his mouth covered hers, and it was like nothing she had ever known. For the first time since she had met Steve, he was not coolly in control. He was shaking, his body trembling with the same hot urgency as her own. His kiss deepened, his tongue erotically probing the honey sweetness of her mouth.

"God, I want you," he groaned, his lips taking hers again and again in short, passionate kisses. He buried his hands in her hair, holding her prisoner while his mouth plundered hers, taking and giving endless pleasure. She responded wildly, completely, as she knew she always would with Steve. There was nothing that he could take that she wouldn't lay gladly at his feet.

She felt a wracking shudder shake him, and suddenly they were both sinking to their knees before the fire and Steve's hands were working deftly at the knot beneath her breasts. The material parted and he slipped the blouse down over her arms to the ground. He was breathing heavily, his eyes intent on the taut, rosy peaks of her breasts. He bent his head slowly and caressed the aroused nipples with his tongue with maddening deliberation. Jenny drew in her breath sharply and he looked up to meet her eyes. His own had a curiously blind look to them as he slowly reached out to bring her dark silky hair over her shoulders to veil her breasts. He pushed her backward until she was lying before him and then his lips were on her breasts, kissing and nipping through the sensuous veil of silk until she was moaning in a frenzy of desire. He was lying beside her now, thigh to thigh, and she could feel the thrusting arousal of his body.

"Jenny, I've got to have you." He groaned and his hands worked frantically at the front zipper of her jeans.

She was still for a long moment, then slowly slid her arms around his neck. "If that's what you want," she said shakily, her eyes meeting his with perfect trust.

His hot burning gaze revealed his torment of need, and then slowly the glazed expression faded from Steve's eyes. His hand reached out to cup her breasts gently. "You'd let me do it, wouldn't you?" he asked huskily. "You'd let me do anything I wanted to you?"

Her silver eyes were serene. "Yes, anything." How could she help surrendering anything that he desired of her? This was Steve. There wasn't a corner of her life that was not filled with her love for him.

He shook his head incredulously and his mouth curved wryly. "I may be a bastard where women are concerned, but you've got me beat. How can I take advantage of such generosity?" He backed away from her, his gaze fixed regretfully on her full, creamy breasts. "I wish to hell I could."

He quickly unbuttoned his shirt and stripped it off. He pulled her to a kneeling position and put her arms in the sleeves, then buttoned the shirt meticulously.

Her hands went out to touch his hair-roughened chest. He was so beautiful, she thought dreamily.

Steve drew in his breath sharply, his muscles tensing at her touch. "No!" he gasped, catching her hands in his. "How much control do you think I have?"

"Considerably more than I do, evidently," she said, her lips quirking.

"Don't be too sure," he said, rising to his feet. "I'm fairly explosive where you're concerned, young lady." He strode toward the car. "Stay where you are," he called over his shoulder as she started to rise.

When he returned, he was carrying a blanket, thermos, and a white crewneck sweater. He draped the red blanket about her shoulders and pulled the sweater over his own head. Then he settled down beside her and opened the thermos, which contained black coffee liberally laced with brandy by the smell of it.

"You came prepared," she said lightly as he handed her the plastic cup. She took a wary sip and then made a face. The well water had been better than this.

"I didn't know what I'd find out here." His lips twisted wryly. "I should have known better than to expect the usual from Jenny Cashman."

"How did you find out where I was?" she asked, taking another sip.

"When you didn't show up for dinner, I went looking for you. It didn't take me long to get it out of that punk kid." There was a fierce pleasure in Steve's face in the flickering firelight.

She shivered. "You didn't hurt him, did you?"

"Not permanently," he said regretfully. "But he's not as pretty as he was the last time you saw him."

"He wasn't looking very appealing to me then, either." She wrinkled her nose with distaste.

His hand tucked a wayward strand of hair behind her ear. "Poor Jenny," he said, a hint of teasing in his voice. "You seem to be acquiring experience by leaps and bounds."

"He said no one would believe that you were my guardian," she burst out, not looking at him.

"He's probably right," Steve said quietly. "Does that bother you?"

Jenny shook her head. "Not if it doesn't matter to you."

"Damn it, it does matter!" he exploded. "I won't have everyone thinking you're some glorified call girl."

"It won't be for long," she said, her voice low. "I'll be moving out as soon as I can find a job."

"And have me going quietly out of my mind wondering what new disaster you'd walked into? No way!" He reached over and took the cup from her and set it forcefully on the ground beside her. He took her hands in his, his eyes compelling. "You're going to have to marry me, Jenny," he said softly.

For a moment she thought she hadn't heard correctly, then she believed she understood. "Because of what happened just now? That's not necessary, Steve. If you want me, then I'll belong to you."

"Damn it, Jenny," he said in exasperation, "will you stop propositioning me? I'm not about to set you up as my mistress and I can't let you go out on your own."

"Marriage is rather a drastic compromise! What if you get tired of me?"

"I haven't gotten tired of you in eight years." He grinned.

"That's different," she said shyly. "I've never gone to bed with you."

"So it naturally follows that I'm going to ravish you and then throw you out of my life? What do you think I am, some kind of satyr?"

She smiled mischievously. "It seems I've heard rumors to that effect."

He touched the tip of her nose with a reproving finger. "Brat," he said succinctly. "Whatever I may be with other women, I'll always put you in a special category."

"Does that mean you'll not be a satyr with me?" She pouted disappointedly.

"Jenny, will you knock it off?" He was clearly losing control again. "I'm making you an honorable proposal."

"It's no wonder you're doing it badly," she said demurely, her silver eyes dancing through their veil of long dark lashes, "you're so used to the other kind."

"Jenny!"

She launched herself at him, her arms sliding around his waist, her head burrowing in his rough knit sweater. "I'm sorry," she whispered. "I'm just so happy. I didn't want to leave you."

His hands moved gently on her hair as he held her tenderly. "Did you think after all the trouble I took raising you that I'd actually let you walk away from me?" he asked huskily.

She looked up at last, her eyes shining with tears. "If you ever do get tired of me, just tell me. I'll go away. I don't ever want to be a bother to you, Steve."

"For God's sake, Jenny. What are you trying to do to me?" he asked gruffly, his eyes suspiciously bright. "Will you just shut up?" His lips touched hers with an infinite gentleness.

He drew a deep breath and put her from him. "Now, if I want to get you back home before dawn, we'd better get on the road." He rose and put out the fire while she folded the blanket and capped the thermos.

When they were finally seated in the Mercedes,

Jenny rolled down the window to take one last look at the desolate streets of the ghost town.

"Are you glad to see the last of it?" Steve asked as he backed and turned the car.

She shook her head, smiling dreamily. "I was just wondering if we could possibly have the wedding here."

"What?" Steve's face held blank surprise as his gaze ran over the tumbledown shacks that comprised Caleb's Gulch. "No, we cannot," he said firmly. Then, as he caught sight of her disappointed face and the wistfulness in her silver eyes, he sighed resignedly. "Would you settle for the first wedding anniversary?"

Six

IT WAS INCREDIBLY easy to marry in Las Vegas. With his usual efficiency, Steve organized the ceremony for two days later. It was to be a private affair with only Joe Magruder and Mike Novacek as witnesses. Pat Marchant, Steve's secretary, was attending to the details of the ceremony, so it only remained for Jenny to find a gown.

It took a long, exhaustive search, but she finally found it. The gown was straight out of the Renaissance, and its low squared neckline, long, tight sleeves, and empire waist turned her into Juliet. Completely free of ornamentation, it relied on its cut and the richness of the taffeta for effect. She wore a simple Juliet cap as a headdress and let her hair flow loose and shining down her back. It was an incredibly romantic look, and it fitted her mood exactly.

"You make me feel like I should be wearing hose and doublet," Steve said wryly as he helped her into the car that evening on the way to the ceremony.

She shook her head decisively. "You're perfect just as you are," she asserted. He was fantastically handsome in the black tux, she thought admiringly.

Steve looked down at the glowing face beside him for a long moment, his blue eyes oddly sad. "You look like the first breath of spring," he said in a low voice. "And you make me feel a hundred years old and lost in wickedness."

She smiled brilliantly, her hand reaching out to cover his on the steering wheel. This was the first really personal remark he'd made to her since they'd returned from Caleb's Gulch. When they'd gotten back to the hotel, it was as if he'd erected a barrier between them. He had been as charming, affectionate, and considerate as one could ask, but try as she would, Jenny couldn't see behind the urbane mask the lover who had ravished her senses.

He looked down at the delicacy of the small hand on his own. "You're everything a bride should be, Jenny," he said with a quiet sincerity that filled her with happiness. Then putting the car in gear, he pulled away.

They were met at the church steps by a surprisingly solemn Mike Novacek. He was taking his duties seriously, Jenny thought in amusement. His eyes widened as he helped her from the car and stood back a pace to look at her. His guttural voice was hoarser than usual as he said, "You look like a princess in a storybook, chicken."

She squeezed his arm affectionately. "That's what I feel like," she said simply. "I'm so happy." She looked him over thoroughly. "You look absolutely fantastic, Mike."

Actually, he was positively debonair and sophisticated in his black tux. The excellent cut of the coat fitted smoothly over his massive shoulders, and the stark black and white discreetly complimented both his size and coloring.

He made a face. "I may not have the panache of a Fred Astaire, but I had to do you proud, Jenny."

She kissed him lightly on the cheek. "Thank you, Mike."

Steve had come around the car and was regarding them indulgently. "Is Joe here yet?" he asked, as he took Jenny's arm.

Mike nodded. "He's waiting inside the church."

Jenny gathered the train of her gown over one arm and with Steve's protective hand on her elbow, she climbed the shallow stairs and entered the vestibule of the church.

Pat Marchant had chosen the church with faultless insight. The small white stone building was exactly what she would have selected herself, Jenny thought contentedly. The chapel reminded her of the tiny country church she had attended in Switzerland with her classmates. The decor was simple and unpretentious, the only ornamental note being the beautiful stained glass windows that were gloriously illuminated by the rays of the setting sun. The altar was banked with masses of colorful spring flowers of every description.

Jenny had never attended a wedding before. It

seemed to her that the ceremony was over in a surprisingly short time, and she was receiving a chaste salute on the cheek from Joe and Mike before she knew it.

"Is that all there is to it?" she whispered to Steve, as they left the chapel. "Are you sure we're married?"

"Quite sure," he said, grinning. "Would you like to go back and do it again?"

"No, once will be enough for me," she said serenely. For all my life, she added to herself.

Steve was surprisingly quiet on the drive back to the hotel, but Jenny made up for it. She seemed to be lit up from within and the words poured out of her in a bubbling stream.

With the impending purchase of another hotel-casino in the offing, it was impossible for Steve to get away for a honeymoon at the present time. He'd promised when the deal was finalized he would take her on the traditional wedding trip, and asked her with some curiosity where she would like to go.

Her answer had been prompt and unequivocal. "Santa Flores."

Steve had made no comment, but there had been

a hint of tenderness in the smile that he gave her. Now she was glad they weren't going away. She wanted only to be alone with Steve in the familiar privacy of their apartment.

When the front door had closed behind them, she turned wordlessly and slipped into his arms with a contented sigh. Steve held her quietly for a long moment before gently pushing her away.

"We have to talk," he said abruptly. "Why don't you go into the living room and fix a drink for me, while I make a telephone call."

He disappeared into the bedroom, leaving her standing there looking after him in amazement. She walked slowly into the living room, a frown creasing her forehead. She pulled off the Juliet cap and dropped it carelessly on the coffee table before going to the bar, where she fixed Steve's bourbon and water and poured a ginger ale for herself.

When Steve returned from the bedroom, she saw he'd removed his jacket and tie and unbuttoned the top button of his white shirt. He crossed to the bar and took the glass from her. "Thank you," he said, quickly taking a long drink. "This isn't going to be easy for me."

She was suddenly frightened. "What's wrong, Steve? Why are you acting like this?"

His eyes were the steel blue of a surgeon's scalpel. "I deceived you, Jenny," he said without emotion. "This isn't going to be a real marriage."

She was shocked. Though she heard his words, it was as if he were speaking in a foreign language that she couldn't comprehend. "I don't understand," she said numbly. "Why would you do that?"

"Damn it, will you stop looking at me like that? I did it to protect you. You haven't any more business out in the world on your own than a newborn babe." He crashed his glass down on the bar. "That night in Caleb's Gulch I realized I had to do something. It was only a matter of time until you tried to leave me and set up on your own. I couldn't allow that."

"You couldn't allow . . ." she echoed stupidly. The hurt was so intense she couldn't think straight.

"Listen, Jenny." His voice was gruff. "I'm too old for you. There's no way a genuine marriage between us could work out. We'll stay married for a few years until you're able to fend for yourself and then get a quiet annulment."

"You have it all planned." She rubbed her forehead in confusion. "Annulment. That means non-consummation, doesn't it?" She was trying to work it out. "That's why no divorce. You said virgins didn't appeal to you."

"Don't be a fool, Jenny," he said savagely. "You know I almost went up in flames the other night at the Gulch. I sure as hell couldn't hide it. You turned me on more than any woman I've ever known."

"Then you're afraid I'll try to tie you down," she concluded dully. "I told you it wouldn't be like that. I know you're not in love with me, but I thought I could at least give you that."

"I know you too well ever to be afraid of your tying me down." He ran his hand distractedly through his dark gold hair. "You're too damned independent in spirit, but you're not equipped to be independent *in fact*. I told you that you've always been special to me. I promised myself a long time ago that I'd always take care of you. I'm not about to take advantage of your youth!"

He took out a cigarette and lit it, regarding her through the smoke with narrowed eyes. "Sure, I could take you to bed and we'd both enjoy it. But you're a loyal little thing, Jenny. Once you'd committed yourself to that extent, you'd find it impossible to repudiate the vows we took this evening. In a couple of years, when you're mature enough to know what you really want, you'd find it hell to walk away. I'm not about to put you in a spot like that."

Nor yourself either, she thought cynically. Steve wanted to take no chances of her forming a permanent romantic attachment for him. "Didn't it occur to you that I might just walk out and get an annulment now, when I found out how you really felt?" she asked bitterly.

He nodded. "It occurred to me," he said coolly. "But I hoped to persuade you to be sensible. After all, we've only to continue on as we have been."

He made it all sound so simple. All she had to do was erase the love and passion that had been building in her for a lifetime. How could she return to being his little sister when she only wanted to be his wife, she wondered wildly.

"You've gone to a great deal of trouble," she said flatly. "This must mean a lot to you."

Steve drew a deep breath, his chest tight and ach-

ing. Just a little longer and she'd accept it and go to her room. Please go away, love. A gypsy waif with forever in her eyes. A sensuous goddess gowned in mist, her lovely breasts warm and naked in his hands. A Renaissance princess gliding toward him down the aisle, her face lit with a radiance that would warm him all the days of his life. They were all Jenny. My God, how could he keep himself from taking her in his arms and never letting her go?

There was a flicker of agonized concern on Steve's face as he saw the dull suffering on her own. He took an impulsive step forward. "Jenny . . ."

This wasn't easy for him, Jenny thought, noticing the paleness of his usually bronze skin and the lines of strain about his mouth. Steve never could bear to hurt her. But somehow the pity in his face made her own pain more achingly sharp.

"I'll stay," she said, her silver eyes desolate, empty. "I owe you that. But only until I finish a secretarial training course and can support myself." She smiled sadly. "That should put your conscience at rest."

"That will do for now," Steve said confidently. "I know you're hurting right now, but you'll find it grows easier. We've been together too long for the strain to remain. You'll see that I'm right."

"Aren't you always?" But not this time. Her mouth twisted in bitterness. This throbbing ache wasn't going to go away.

He kissed her gently on the forehead. "Go to bed. You'll feel better in the morning."

She nodded. He was treating her like a sick child, she thought wearily. Take two aspirins and see me in the morning. Was there enough aspirin in the world to dull this pain?

"Good night, Steve." She turned and walked silently to her room.

In the next few months Jenny found that though the ache never entirely disappeared, it did, as Steve had predicted, get better. She found they could act and talk with a guarded friendliness toward each other she'd not believed possible on that ghastly wedding night. If their eyes were often wary and if they cautiously avoided any physical contact, it was surely to be expected.

She'd enrolled in a secretarial course at a local

business college the day following the wedding. It was blessedly hard work and engrossed her complete attention for at least the major part of the daylight hours. In the evening she went to her room immediately after dinner and did her homework. Steve usually went out in the evenings now. She didn't ask him where he went or with whom, nor did he volunteer the information.

She worked late trying desperately to exhaust herself, for she found the time directly before sleep the most excruciating. She seemed to be more vulnerable then. She was flooded by thoughts and emotions that she carefully guarded against during the day. Desire, regret, loneliness, they all played on her nerves until she felt physically ill.

The overwork and lack of sleep had their inevitable effect. She began to lose weight and dark circles appeared under her eyes. She was so lethargic that even Mike's superb meals couldn't tempt her appetite. It was Jenny's refusal of breakfast for the second time in a week that led to Mike's final explosion.

"That's it, I've had enough!" He slapped the rejected plate down on the table with a resounding thud. Jenny looked up from her coffee, startled. Mike pointed a commanding finger at her. "Stay right where you are," he ordered. He vanished into the kitchen to bring out a pot of coffee and a second cup and saucer. He filled the cup, set the pot on the table, and sat down next to her.

"We're going to talk," he said firmly. "I've stood by for three months and kept my peace, but now I've had it. When you start refusing my strawberry crepes, something has to be done."

Jenny hid a smile of amusement. "I'm just not hungry this morning," she soothed.

"You weren't hungry yesterday morning, either," Mike said accusingly. "You picked at your food last night at dinner." He closed a huge hand around her slender wrist. "Look at that." His tone was disgusted. "You must have lost ten pounds in the last month."

"I'll gain it back. I'm just working rather hard right now."

"Too hard. You and Steve are both acting crazy."

"I'd rather not talk about it," she said reservedly, pushing back her chair.

"Just sit still, Jenny. You're not going anywhere

until I've had my say." Mike released her wrist and picked up his cup. "Steve has been taut as a bow string ever since that blasted wedding and I'm tired of walking on eggs around him."

"It's your imagination," she said lightly. "I haven't noticed any change."

"He's edgy as a beestung bear. Oh, he makes an effort around you to appear the same, but the rest of us are catching hell."

"Well, then perhaps you'd better take it up with him," she suggested, looking down at her cup.

He gave a derisive snort. "Do you think I'm nuts? Steve doesn't tolerate interference from anyone."

"Exactly!" she said, looking up to meet his eyes. "So why come to me?"

"Because the same thing that's bothering him is messing you up, too," he said in exasperation.

"No, you're wrong there." She looked back down at her cup. "I can guarantee that we're not suffering from the same complaint."

"Well, something pretty close," he said shrewdly. "It sure has the same symptoms, and I'd bet the same medicine would cure it."

Jenny was silent, afraid the tears that were so

close would show in her voice if she spoke. All she needed was to break down in front of Mike.

He covered her hand with his own gigantic paw, his hazel eyes gentle. "Look, kid, I know it's none of my business, but the whole thing makes me mad as blazes. The night you got married you were practically incandescent. You could have lit up the whole Las Vegas strip with that smile of yours. I came back to the apartment two days later and you'd both closed up inside." An uncomfortable flush stained his cheeks. "You're just a baby, Jenny, and you've never had a woman to talk to," he said awkwardly. "I know that sometimes for a woman the first time can be painful, but you shouldn't let it turn you off. Sex can be a helluva lot of fun."

It would have been impossible for Mike not to realize she and Steve still occupied separate bedrooms, and that theirs was not a normal marriage, but he'd never commented on it. Now Jenny was torn apart by conflicting emotions. She was touched by Mike's caring enough to broach a subject that was obviously embarrassing to him, and felt a hysterical desire to laugh at his total misreading of the situation.

Two tears rolled slowly down her cheeks. "I wouldn't know about that," she admitted in a muffled voice.

There was a stunned expression on Mike's craggy features as he pursed his lips in a soundless whistle. "I never figured on that. Not with Steve Jason."

"Well, you should have," Jenny said bitterly. "He says I'm in a special category." Then her face crumpled and the tears fell in earnest. "Oh, Mike, I'm so miserable."

He gazed at her helplessly while she struggled to halt the tears. When she finally managed to control herself, he silently handed her a napkin and she wiped her face like a woeful little girl.

"Why the hell did Steve marry you?"

"He wanted to protect me." She gave a short laugh. "I was getting into too much trouble."

"He was really wild that day you went to Hoover," Mike said thoughtfully.

She nodded. "That's when he made up his mind that I had to be protected against the world," she said caustically. "But he tells me that in a few years I *may* be mature enough to care for myself, and then we'll get an annulment." She shrugged. "I find

I'm not that much of a glutton for punishment. After I finish this business course, I'm getting out."

He nodded absently. "I can see how you'd want to. You've been nuts about him for years." His hazel eyes were absorbed in thought.

She smiled wryly. "I've never been able to hide it."

Mike's eyes flicked to life suddenly, and he leaned forward and took her hand again. "I think you're throwing in the towel too soon, Jenny."

She squeezed his hand. "I can't make Steve fall in love with me."

"I don't know about that," Mike admitted, grinning. "We might take a stab at that, too. But I do know that you already have the makings of a damn good marriage if you both work at it. Hell, kid, you two have got it all. Companionship, trust, mutual respect, admiration. The ingredients are all there. All you have to do is blend them properly."

"This isn't a recipe for one of your famous cakes, Mike," she said dryly.

He shrugged. "Same principle." His eyes were serious. "Steve is a very complex guy, and he's been a loner all his life. He's tough as hell and can't stand the thought of relying on anyone but himself. That's a pretty heavy combination to try to beat, but you have a good shot at it, Jenny."

She felt a swift rising of hope. "Why do you say that?" she asked cautiously.

"Because he cares for you already. He must care a hell of a lot for you to take such a drastic step just to keep you safe."

Jenny grinned. Marriage for Mike would be the ultimate in sacrifice.

He smiled sheepishly. "Not that you aren't a sexy little morsel, Jenny."

"I understand, Mike," she laughed, her eyes dancing.

"Like I said," he went on, "you've got an edge. You've just got to work on him."

"I suppose you've got some suggestions on that, too," she said, her spirits suddenly soaring.

He shook his head. "Nope," he said, grinning. "It's your battle, I leave it to you to choose the artillery." He rose to his feet. "Think about it," he suggested, and vanished into the kitchen.

Jenny thought about it. She went through the day in a daze. Her typing was atrocious, her shorthand unreadable. Her mind kept chewing on Mike's words relentlessly. She'd been in such a hopeless morass that it was hard to take in the possibility she really had a chance of winning Steve's love. But the more she thought about it, the clearer it became to her. She felt an impatient disgust at her former hopeless discouragement. She'd never been a quitter before. Why had she given up so easily in this instance when all her future happiness was at stake? Mike was right. She had a chance. It was up to her to turn that possibility into a reality.

SEVEN

ONCE THE RESOLUTION was made Jenny only had to form a plan and initiate it. She set to work like a general planning his campaign. The battle Mike had spoken about would be more like a full-scale war, she thought grimly. Steve wasn't about to surrender after one skirmish. The first thing to do was to analyze her opponent's weaknesses, which wasn't an easy thing to do with a man as tough as Steve Jason. But according to Mike, she herself was one of those weaknesses. Steve genuinely liked her and also was extremely protective and possessive where she was concerned. There might be something she could use in that. In addition, Steve was a very passionate and virile man and he'd already admitted that she could turn him on.

She was left with a three-part strategy. One, regain lost ground by getting their relationship back to the warm, easy status it was before Caleb's Gulch. Two, seduction. Three, use Steve's possessiveness as a lever. She was vague as to how the last was to be accomplished in order to move him from his stubbornly avuncular position, but she was sure something would occur to her.

One.

Jenny quietly slipped into her seat at the breakfast table early the next morning. Steve looked up in surprise, his blue eyes wary. Jenny had been purposely avoiding his company before, waiting until she knew he'd left for the office before coming out of her room for her own breakfast.

"Good morning," she said lightly, giving him a warm smile as she seated herself opposite him, unfolding her napkin briskly.

"Good morning. What gets you up so early?"

"I just thought it had been a long time since we breakfasted together," she said calmly. Then, as

Mike came in from the kitchen, "Hi, Mike, what have you got for us this morning?"

"Pancakes," Mike said with a grin. "Think you can force some down?"

"Bring them on, I'm starved," she said enthusiastically.

Throughout the meal she kept up a running conversation. It was surprisingly easy to be friendly and natural with Steve. Now that she was committed to her course of action, the strain was miraculously gone. She genuinely liked Steve's company at all times, and now she could relax and enjoy herself.

Her attitude couldn't help but influence his own, and Steve's tension gradually eased. By the time he'd finished his coffee, he was teasing her much as he had before that disastrous wedding night.

He'd stared in amazement as she had put away three pancakes and then cheerfully asked Mike for another. "You must have been starved," he commented dryly.

"I've lost some weight lately," Jenny answered. "I'm trying to gain it back."

"In one meal?"

"It's very important. I'm in training," she said serenely, pouring syrup on the pancake.

"Training for what?"

"Just training," she said with an enigmatic smile.

Jenny's behavior for the next two weeks closely followed the pattern of that first day. She got up every morning to have breakfast with Steve. When he came home to dinner, she was both warm and affectionate, the perfect companion. He was fast losing his defensiveness with her. She counted it a major victory when he stayed home one evening and played backgammon with her, displaying all the signs of enjoyment.

She hadn't forgotten the strategy for her next objective while pursuing this course of action, but had to set it on the back burner while she made preparation for its inception. Since it was the most important part of her campaign, she had to acquire sufficient ammunition.

She cut her class time to only morning hours and spent the afternoons shopping. She used Steve's charge accounts with ruthless abandon, smothering a guilty twinge or two with the firm self-admonition that it was really for Steve's own good. By the time

the two weeks had elapsed, she had the most alluring and just plain sexy wardrobe imaginable, and
she was ready for the second step.

Two.

It took Jenny two hours to dress and fifteen minutes to get up her nerve that first morning. When
she arrived in the breakfast room, Steve had not yet
appeared.

Mike was setting the table when she strolled with
seeming carelessness to her seat. When he looked
up, he did a double take, and then gave a low whistle. "Where did you get that? Frederick's of Holly-
wood?" he asked, grinning.

She made a face. "I'll have you know, it's a French
original." She frowned uncertainly. "Do you think
it's too much?"

He looked at the rose chiffon negligee critically,
his eyes lingering on the extreme décolletage. "Too
much it definitely isn't," he said dryly. "Steve may
argue it's not enough."

"You know what I mean. Is it too obvious?"

"It's in good taste," Mike assured her, his eyes
twinkling. "But there's no way of revealing that
much skin without being obvious."

She had to be satisfied with that. When Steve entered the room, he didn't do a double take as Mike had, but his mouth tightened ominously. He said nothing, however, and seated himself opposite her with a brief "Good morning."

Jenny was disappointed but hid it carefully. She chattered happily through the meal and tried to be as natural as possible. Steve was unusually silent, and she was happy to note he seemed to have a great deal of trouble keeping his eyes off the cleavage revealed by the negligee. He didn't comment on her attire until he was rising to leave.

"I gather you're not going to school today," he said, his eyes raking the filmy draperies of the negligee.

She shrugged. "I thought I'd take a few weeks off. Mike says I've been overdoing it."

"He's probably right," he said absently, his eyes on the neckline of her gown again. "That's new, isn't it?"

She touched the bodice lightly. "I decided everything in my wardrobe was a bit too childish now that I've become a matron," she said, smiling demurely. "I didn't want everyone to think you'd robbed the cradle."

His eyebrows lifted mockingly. "That little number suggests more a mistress than a matron."

"Oh, do you really think so?" she asked with naive pleasure. "That's even more sophisticated, isn't it?"

Steve muttered a curse and strode out of the room.

Jenny smiled with profound satisfaction. Her first foray had been an unqualified success.

She didn't rest on her laurels in the days that followed. No ancient harem beauty spent more time and effort than she in preparing for her encounters with Steve. Her hair and makeup were works of art, but her wardrobe was the pièce de résistance. In the morning she wore flimsy negligees, and in the evening her sophisticated lounging clothes were, if anything, even more revealing than the lingerie.

Jenny never made the mistake of being coy or acting the femme fatale. She had a shrewd notion that her lack of experience would tend to make her more ludicrous than seductive in that role. She did, however, set up a few situations where she was forced to brush against Steve or lean close enough to him so that he could smell the scent of her new perfume that the salesclerk had described as madly exciting.

The first time it had happened, Steve had drawn in his breath sharply, his body tensing involuntarily at the contact. After that, he was careful to show no emotion, except in the tightening of his lips and a stormy impatience in the electric blue eyes. On the whole, Jenny was quite pleased with the results of her efforts. Steve was becoming gratifyingly aware of her as a woman, if his singularly bad temper was any sign.

Steve's irritation reached its peak one evening the following week. She was waiting for him in the living room, as she did every evening now, and flipping through a magazine when she heard the front door close. He usually went directly to his room to wash up before dinner and tonight was no exception. Jenny crossed swiftly to the bar and had time to make him a drink before he appeared in the arched doorway of the living room. She turned on the stool, holding out his glass with a bright smile.

It was not returned. Steve's lips thinned and his

eyes flickered dangerously as his gaze ran over her. He crossed the room swiftly and took the drink from her hand. He drank half of it in one swallow, then lowered it to regard her sourly.

"Don't you ever wear a bra?" he asked sarcastically, staring at the gold jersey halter top whose clinging material left nothing to the imagination. She'd been very pleased with that top when she found it in a small specialty department at I. Magnin's. High in the front, the top plunged daringly to the waist in the back.

"No," she said simply. "I find them uncomfortable, and the saleswoman said I didn't really need one." She reached for the bottle of ginger ale, turning her back on him deliberately to let him get the full effect of the halter. She heard a hastily indrawn breath, but she ignored him serenely as she added ice to her glass and poured the ginger ale over it. She was just preparing to turn back to him when she felt his hand on her naked flesh. She froze, her breath stopping, as his fingers rubbed sensuously at the small of her back. It was as if he were stroking her with a live electric wire.

"It feels like satin," he said hoarsely. Jenny forced

herself to turn and face him. His eyes were glazed and his face flushed as his gaze fixed compulsively on the front of her top. Her cheeks turned a bright scarlet as she realized that her own arousal was as blatantly displayed as if she wore nothing at all.

His hand reached out slowly, his face intent. She held her breath, feeling as if she were drowning. In the last second before he touched her enticing breasts, he wrenched himself away with a muttered curse.

His voice was hard when he spoke again, but she could see the pulse that still throbbed revealingly in his temple. "Would you like to tell me what the hell you think you're doing?"

She drew a shaking breath. It was one thing to scheme and plan to reach her objective. It was yet another to actually confront Steve's sexual magnetism. She played for time and picked up the ginger ale that she'd almost forgotten. "I'm just making myself a drink," she said lightly.

Steve's blue eyes narrowed dangerously. "Don't be obtuse," he said bluntly. "I'm not stupid, Jenny. I've watched you play your little games for over a week now, and I'm pretty fed up."

There was a barely controlled tension in his voice that intimidated her in spite of her resolution. "I don't know what you mean," she stalled, taking a sip of her drink.

He cursed again. "I want to know why I'm being given the treatment," he said grimly. "I've been vamped before by women with a good deal more experience than you. I believe I can recognize the technique."

"I'm sure you can," she said, moistening her lips with her tongue nervously. She looked up to see his gaze fixed on her lips in fascination, then he dragged it away. He drained the rest of his drink in one swallow and started to make himself another.

"Well, are you going to enlighten me as to why I'm being given this two-shows-a-day striptease?" he asked caustically. "I've begun to make bets with myself as to what new portion of your anatomy I'll be allowed to view each day."

The color flooded back to her cheeks, but Jenny knew she mustn't let him disconcert her. "I've decided I don't like the idea of an annulment," she said clearly. "I'd rather be divorced."

Steve went still. "Would you mind clarifying that statement," he asked carefully.

"I'm tired of being the chaste little girl," she replied, not looking at him. "I've decided that I want to become experienced."

"And by experienced I assume you mean in the carnal sense?" he asked politely.

Jenny nodded, her face growing redder by the minute.

"And I've been chosen to initiate you?"

She nodded again. "I thought it would be more practical to choose someone I'm familiar with." She tried to keep her voice cool and level. "And, after all, we *are* married."

"I suppose I should be honored," he said softly.

"Well, flattered, perhaps," she agreed. "You must admit that you have an excellent reputation in that area."

The blue eyes were no longer flickering but blazing, and his voice was hoarse with rage. "Damn you!" he exploded.

This was more difficult than she'd ever imagined. "Does that mean you're turning me down?" she asked lightly, trying to ignore his anger.

"You're damned right I am. And the sooner you get this crazy notion out of your head, the better. If those are the kinds of ideas you're picking up at that school of yours, you can quit right now!"

"Well, I can't help but be aware that I'm probably the only virgin left in the entire town of Las Vegas," she said, grimacing. "It's not at all fashionable."

"Too bad," Steve said through his teeth. "But you'll just have to put up with it."

"Perhaps." She smiled tantalizingly. "But you won't mind if I try to change your mind, will you?"

"You can do your damndest," he said, his face implacable. "You're backing a losing hand, Jenny."

"How can you be sure of that until you've seen my cards?"

He made a strangled exclamation and stalked out of the room.

In the following week Jenny continued her campaign as if the confrontation had never taken place. Steve didn't try to avoid her as she thought he might. He showed up meticulously for breakfast and dinner, treating her with a careful courtesy that was designed to show her how little he was affected by her tactics. She sailed on her course placidly, and if anything her wardrobe became even more daring and her demeanor frankly alluring. Steve's manner gradually became more and more irate, and when one evening at dinner she looked up to meet a gaze that was nakedly hungry, Jenny sighed in sheer delight.

His face clouded stormily as he met the satisfaction in her eyes and with a muttered curse, he flung his napkin violently on the table and strode out of the room. Jenny stared after him, a beatific smile on her face.

Mike, who had been a witness to the silent exchange, grinned wickedly. "Our Mr. Jason isn't used to denying himself."

"Then he'd better alter the situation," she said calmly.

Mike looked at her speculatively. "You're a very tough lady, Jenny."

She made a face at him. "I have to be. Steve Jason is no pussycat."

He was more like a tiger, she thought gloomily, more than a week later. She was stretched out by the pool sunbathing in a white vinyl lounge chair, and the subject gnawing at her mind was the usual perplexing one. She'd made no progress at all in the last week. Steve might be frustrated, but he was also awesomely stubborn. She rolled over on her back and adjusted her sunglasses.

"Hi, mermaid."

She looked up, seeing only a dark silhouette against the sun. "Rex?" She scrambled into a sitting position and ripped off her sunglasses.

"None other," Rex Brody replied.

"What are you doing here?" she asked, pleased. "I thought you were on the road."

"Tours don't last forever, you know. It's been four months. I open at the Pagan Room again tomorrow night."

He looked exactly the same, Jenny thought, except for the dark circles under his eyes and the weary lines about the sensual mouth. "You look tired," she said.

Rex ran his hand through his dark, glossy hair. "Those one nighters are really bummers." He made a face. "Every time I swear I'll never do another tour, then they up the money and I give in again."

"I shouldn't think you'd have to worry about money, Rex," she said lightly.

"We all have to worry about money," he said with a laugh. "Except maybe you, mermaid." He knelt beside her and picked up her left hand, regarding the diamond-encrusted wedding ring critically. "Very nice. No engagement ring?"

"There wasn't time," she answered. "It was all very sudden."

"So I understand," he said softly. "Why did you do it, Jenny? He's rich as Croesus, but I don't think that would influence you."

She shook her head. "The usual reason," she said. "I've loved Steve Jason as long as I can remember."

He grinned boyishly. "I thought you were an old fashioned girl. I must admit I had an idea there was something in the wind before I left."

She looked up in confusion. "I don't see how you could," she said ruefully. "I certainly didn't!"

"Your husband nearly took me apart after that party at Danny Smith's. Verbally, that is." He rubbed his jaw thoughtfully. "For a while it was touch and go whether it was going to be physically, too."

Jenny took his hand in her own, her eyes distressed. "I'm so sorry, Rex. I tried to tell him none of it was your fault."

Rex shook his head, his dark eyes serious. "No, he was right. I should never have taken you there. I knew you had no business in a place like that, but I thought I could take care of you." He grimaced. "Well, I sure blew that." Looking down at their linked hands, he continued, "I tried calling several times to apologize, but I always got the brush-off from the guy who answered the phone. Miss Cashman was never in to Mr. Brody."

Mike, Jenny thought in exasperation. "I didn't know," she said. "I wouldn't have refused your calls, Rex."

He gave her an endearingly crooked smile. "I didn't think you would. I like you, Jenny. I don't have many friends. It's a phony world I live in and it's hard to tell the real from the mirage. But you're real, Jenny."

"Thank you," she said huskily, touched by his

sincerity. "I like you, too, Rex, and I think you'd be a very good friend."

His black eyes twinkled mischievously. "Don't say that too loudly," he joked. "You'll ruin my reputation as a swinger."

She giggled. "I imagine you're well able to maintain that image," she said, thinking back to the first day she'd met him.

"I manage," he admitted breezily. Then he was grave again. "Seriously, Jenny, I'd like to be friends with you if you can forgive me that mess at Danny's." He paused. "I'd even like to be friends with that intimidating husband of yours."

"That's very generous of you," she said, grinning.

Rex shook his head. "Steve Jason is real, too," he explained simply. "I guess I respect that more than any other quality. The ability to stay true to yourself in spite of all the phoniness around you." For a moment his dark eyes were curiously lost and empty.

"You're not phony, Rex," she said gently.

"Not now." His voice was quiet. "But I have been in the past, and it would be easy to slide back into it again." He touched her cheek lightly. "That's why I need to be around people like you. To remind myself that it's only my world that's papier-mâché."

He rose lithely to his feet, his demeanor changing with the quicksilver swiftness that she was beginning to become accustomed to. "I've got a rehearsal in fifteen minutes. Are you coming to see me? I'll be performing here for another two weeks."

"I wouldn't miss it," she assured him.

He gave her a casual wave and strode off, his bearing invulnerably debonair.

Jenny gazed after him with warm liking. She was going to enjoy being friends with Rex Brody, she mused. Perhaps she would invite Rex to dinner so Steve could see how much more there was to the singer than appeared on the surface. Maybe they could find a nice girl to introduce him to. Preferably one under six feet, she thought with a reminiscent grin.

Abruptly she came to her senses. With the status quo of her marriage at the moment, there was no way she could attempt a reconciliation between Steve and Rex Brody. She remembered Steve's condemnation of Rex that night after the show in the Pagan Room, and then with a quickening pulse, the passionate scene that followed.

Suddenly she caught her breath and her silver eyes came to brilliant life. That was it! It was right there before her and she'd almost missed it. Number three!

Eight

Three.

Once the idea had taken hold, Jenny was eager to organize its inception. She hurriedly slipped into her robe and returned to the apartment. In forty-five minutes she had showered, dressed, and was on her way down to the foyer.

She had no problem gaining entrance to the Pagan Room. The security guards all knew her as Steve's wife and that gave her access to anywhere in the hotel that she chose to go. She quietly seated herself at a ringside table and waited patiently until Rex had finished rehearsing.

He strolled over to the table, wiping his brow

with a towel. He slung it around his neck and, turning a chair around, straddled it casually, resting his arms on the back. "When I asked you to come to see the show, I didn't realize you'd be so eager," he teased. "It's really much better in costume."

"I want you to do me a favor," she said directly, and proceeded to tell him what she wanted him to do.

When she'd finished. Rex whistled. "Do you want to get me killed?" he said, half joking. "Making Steve Jason jealous could be a very dangerous game, mermaid."

"I'd never let him hurt you," she promised. "And I'll explain everything later."

"I assume you have a good reason for this little plot," he said reluctantly. "I didn't think you played these little games." There was a touch of disappointment in his dark eyes.

"I don't," Jenny said quietly. "This isn't a game, Rex. It may save my marriage." She'd hoped to avoid confiding the reason for her plea, but she could see now that she owed it to him if she expected to receive his help.

She briefly outlined the circumstances of her marriage and her subsequent attempts to make it a real one. When she'd finished, she noticed to her profound displeasure that Rex was struggling desperately not to laugh. When he caught sight of her offended expression, he gave up the battle and collapsed into whoops of laughter.

"I'm sorry, Jenny," he gasped finally, wiping his eyes. "But the idea of you as a wicked seductress is a little too much."

She smiled reluctantly. "Not wicked," she corrected. "I was aiming more at wholesome seduction."

"I recognize the distinction," he said solemnly, then started to laugh again.

"Will you stop that," Jenny said indignantly. "I was very good at it!"

He finally sobered and reached over and patted her hand. "I'm sure you were, little Jenny." He grinned. "You must have put Jason over hot coals."

"Not hot enough, evidently," she said. She looked up at him pleadingly. "Will you help me?"

Rex sighed. "It's against my better judgment. I have a feeling that husband of yours is going to mangle my beautiful profile." Then, as she was about to speak, he put his hand over her lips. "However," he said judiciously, his eyes twinkling, "my contract with him states clearly that he still has to pay my fee if I'm disabled by injury suffered on his premises."

"Nothing like that is going to happen!"

He gave her a wry smile. "You're an innocent, Jenny. Anything could happen in a situation like the one you're setting up." Then as the silver eyes grew troubled, he relented. "Don't worry about it," he said lightly. "I'm probably overreacting. When do you want to set up your little scenario?"

"I thought perhaps three days from now. It would give me time to prepare the way," she said seriously. "Can you get out of the second show on Friday night?"

"I'll manage."

Jenny rose to her feet. She hesitated a moment, then bent swiftly and placed a light kiss on his cheek. "Thank you," she whispered and turned and walked quickly away.

That night Jenny wasn't in the living room when Steve came home. She waited until a full twenty minutes had gone by before she wandered in leisurely.

"Hi, Steve," she said casually. She went to the bar and poured herself her usual ginger ale and crossed to the sofa. Tucking her denim-clad leg beneath her, she curled into the corner and took a sip of her drink. Looking up, she surprised a look of stunned amazement on Steve's face before he quickly masked it. She hid a smile and reached for a fashion magazine on the coffee table.

"What new game are we playing tonight?" he asked dryly, his eyes running over the tailored cotton shirt, jeans, and her face devoid of makeup. "You'll forgive me if I don't know the rules."

"No game at all," she said, smiling warmly at him. "You've won again, as you always do."

"You seem very happy about it," he noted suspiciously.

"I'm not a bit happy about it." Her gray eyes were direct. "But I have to recognize the fact that you have a right to make your own choices." She paused. "Just as I have the right to make mine."

Mike called them to dinner then. Throughout the meal she was conscious of Steve's frequent glances, but she steadily ignored them and continued to converse cheerfully until Mike served coffee.

Steve watched her guardedly as she stirred her coffee, then as she looked up with a bright smile. "I'm sorry if I made you uncomfortable," she said. "I guess I was pretty much of a pest."

He smiled lazily. "It wasn't all that bad. I must admit you can be quite something when you turn on the voltage."

"Something you didn't want," she said sadly. "Well, I promise you that I won't embarrass you again, Steve."

A frown wrinkled his forehead. "You didn't embarrass me, Jenny." He smiled reluctantly. "You certainly kept me on my toes."

She took a sip of coffee, then stood up. "I'm glad you're being so understanding," she said sweetly, heading toward the door.

"And I'm glad you're being sensible again," he said, his smile complacent.

She turned back, her eyebrow arched inquiringly. "Sensible?"

"Giving up that asinine idea of yours about gaining experience."

Her answering smile was full of loving kindness. "Oh, I didn't give up that idea, Steve," she said gently. "Just the one about gaining it from *you*." She turned and left the room.

The next evening she was in the living room, similarly attired, putting a record on the stereo when Steve stormed into the room. She turned in surprise as he took the record from her hands and pushed her into a chair. His face was a set mask of fury.

"What were you doing at Brody's rehearsal yesterday afternoon?"

She couldn't hide the shock she felt. How had he known she'd seen Rex? "He invited me," she stammered. "How did you know I was there?"

"You're not very practiced in intrigue, Jenny," he said savagely, his eyes blazing. "You didn't even try to cover your movements. Don't you know that there's always someone ready to carry tales to the husband when the story is juicy enough?"

"No, I didn't realize that," she said thoughtfully.

"How do you think I felt when I learned that my wife was openly kissing another man?"

She was staring absently at his taut, angry face. Now that she'd recovered from the surprise, she realized here was an added bonus that could be twisted to her advantage. "I can see that it must have been humiliating for you," she said meekly.

"Humiliating! Is that all you've got to say?" he raged. "You kissed that bastard in front of the entire orchestra!"

Jenny had forgotten her grateful salute. It had evidently been blown up into a torrid embrace. She smiled angelically. "You're upset, let me get you a drink." She started to rise.

He pushed her back in the chair. "I don't want a drink," he said through his teeth. "I want an explanation."

She shrugged. "I'm sure the whole thing has been exaggerated. It was all perfectly innocent."

"Brody doesn't have innocent relations with women," Steve snapped. He ran his hand through his golden hair. "I should never have renewed his contract."

"You're overreacting," she said soothingly. "It won't happen again. I promise to be much more discreet in the future."

"You're not going to see him again."

She was silent, regarding him steadily.

"Jenny!" he prompted menacingly.

"I like Rex Brody," she said honestly. "You have no right to interfere in this, Steve."

"I have every right." His hands captured her shoulders. "You're my wife."

"Merely a convenience, remember?" she said with a false lightness.

"I married you to protect you. And men like Brody are what I'm protecting you from."

"And if I don't want to be protected?" she asked softly, her lashes veiling her eyes.

"Too damn bad." His grip on her tightened. "Then I'll just have to protect you from yourself, won't I?"

"That would be a difficult thing to do."

"I think I'm capable of handling one small girl," he said. The electric blue eyes narrowed. "Don't fight me, Jenny. I'm about at the end of my patience."

She shivered involuntarily. Steve's body was as tense as a panther ready to spring, his eyes blazing with emotion.

"We won't fight about it," she agreed, not committing herself.

That Steve noticed the evasion was evidenced by the tightening of his lips, but he said no more.

The silence continued between them for the next two days. But though Steve's manner was carefully casual, Jenny was conscious that his attention was on her with unnerving watchfulness.

On Friday she dressed as carefully as a matador preparing to enter the bullring. The gown she wore had one quite obvious purpose. Meant to entice and seduce, it was incredibly successful at both objectives. It was a deep glowing red, a color which she had always avoided because it was a bit spectacular with her olive skin and dark hair. The fabric, a soft silk jersey that seemed to invite the touch, was fashioned into a simple sheath that was shockingly form-fitting and slit to mid-thigh in front. The simple décolleté was so constructed that it cupped her breasts lovingly, accenting the cleavage, and baring an alluring expanse of gleaming golden flesh.

She made up with great care, accenting her eyes, glossing her lips to a luscious pink. She briefly considered putting up her hair, thinking it would make her look more sophisticated, but finally decided to leave it down. She brushed it until it gleamed with a satin sheen, then drew it forward to nestle provocatively on the rise of her breasts. She smiled happily as she looked at her reflection in the mirror. She looked positively dangerous, she thought with satisfaction.

She tripped jauntily through to the kitchen. Mike was standing by the stove with his back to her, and she tapped him lightly on the shoulder. "Look at me," she demanded flippantly. "I'm absolutely gorgeous."

He turned, and his eyes widened as they went over her. "That's not all you are," he said dryly. "You're a walking invitation to trouble."

She smiled. "I thought so, too."

"I gather this is part of your battle plan," he drawled.

"With any luck it may be the last engagement."

"You're sure you know what you're doing, fooling around with that Brody guy?" he asked doubtfully. "Steve gave me orders that I was to let him know if Brody tried to get in touch with you."

"That's exactly what I want you to do," she said. "Just tell him when he comes in that I'm meeting Rex for dinner."

"And may I ask where you're having dinner?"

"Why in Rex's suite, of course," she replied smoothly.

"I should have known." Mike groaned. "I can see the fireworks now."

"Me, too," she said happily.

"I hope you don't get more than you bargain for, kid," he said in a soft voice. "You've got Steve in such a state he's ready to explode. Be careful you don't get caught in the blast."

She wrinkled her nose. "I just plan to stage a small explosion. I'll cool it down before it gets out of hand."

"I'm glad you're so confident," he said. "Personally, I wouldn't want to take that chance."

"Wish me luck?" she pleaded, her eyes suddenly solemn.

"Sure," he said gruffly. "You'll need it."

Jenny refused to let Mike's warnings dampen her spirits. Fifteen minutes later she was ringing the bell to Rex's suite.

He opened the door, took one look at her, then groaned. "Man, am I in trouble!"

She smiled saucily. "Is that always your reaction when a woman rings your doorbell?"

"It is when she's Steve Jason's wife," he said gloomily.

She looked him over critically. His dark good looks were set off spectacularly by a faultless white dinner jacket. "You look very good," she said approvingly.

"And you look completely 'bad,'" he said, tongue in cheek. "I guess we've both achieved our objective."

"Do I get to come in?"

He threw the door open wide. "Step into my parlor," he invited. "Though, in this case, that should be your line."

The table in the dining alcove was set with a fine damask cloth and was gleaming with silver and sparkling crystal bathed in the soft candleglow. The room looked quite satisfyingly romantic, Jenny thought, as she dropped her wrap on the couch and went around the room switching off lights strategically.

Rex leaned lazily against the closed door, his arms folded across his chest, and watched her, grinning. "I must call you in when I stage my next seduction. Where do you get your expertise?"

"The late, late show," she replied absently, critically surveying her handiwork.

She looked up indignantly at Rex's snort of laughter. "You're not taking this seriously enough," she said severely.

"Sorry." He grinned unrepentantly. "I'll try to mend my ways. Shall we dine?"

She nodded briskly, and he seated her with scrupulous courtesy. They served themselves from the silver chafing dishes. Jenny ate with a hearty appetite, conversing cheerfully as Rex watched her intently.

"I hope you find the menu suitable," he said slyly, ebony eyes gleaming.

"What?" She looked up, surprised. "Oh, yes, it's very good," she said politely.

"You'll notice, I even ordered oysters."

"Oysters?" she asked, gray eyes puzzled.

"Never mind." He sighed, his lips quirking. "That must not have been on the late, late show."

As they neared the end of the meal, she was checking her watch frequently.

"Isn't he a little behind schedule?" Rex asked.

Jenny shook her head. "Dinner is always late on Fridays. Steve likes to personally greet the high rollers and VIPs who fly in for the weekend."

"Would you like coffee?" he offered, "or shall I ply you with demon rum?"

"The latter, I think," she answered, grinning. "It's more in character."

While he was at the bar she wandered to the low couch. He strolled over to her and handed her a glass. "Screwdriver, very weak," he said. "I want you to have all your wits about you if I need to call on you to protect me." He joined her on the couch, taking a swallow of his own whiskey and water. He looked at her resignedly. "I don't suppose you'd care to put your wrap back on?" he suggested.

She looked up questioningly.

"I'm not used to thinking of women platonically," he explained, his lips twisting wryly. "I'm finding all this bounty well nigh irresistible." His hand moved in compulsive fascination to rub gently at her satin shoulder.

"Get your hands off her, Brody." The voice was laden with menace, and they both looked up startled. Steve stood in the open doorway. Jenny had seen him once before like this, that afternoon at Danny Smith's. But tonight he was more than dangerous; he was deadly.

Rex jumped away from her like a scalded cat before he regained his cool aplomb. "Don't you believe in knocking, Jason?" he asked lightly.

Steve pocketed the master key with which he'd opened the door, and strode forward pantherlike. "You have something that belongs to me. I'm not about to observe the usual amenities," he said savagely.

He had reached the couch and, grasping Jenny by the wrist, hauled her to her feet. His grip was merciless and she gave an involuntary cry of pain.

Rex stiffened. "Now see here, Jason . . ."

"Shut up!" Steve interrupted harshly, his eyes like blue flames. His gaze went over Jenny slowly, his face darkening more by the second. His hand reached out and touched the low bodice. "I guess I don't have to ask what you're doing here," he said, his hand tightening agonizingly on her wrist. "That gown tells it all."

Jenny's eyes flooded with tears. This wasn't the way she had planned it, she thought wildly. He wasn't supposed to be this angry. She wasn't supposed to be this frightened.

"Please," she gasped, trying to wrench her arm away. "You're hurting me."

"Good," he said with savage satisfaction. "I enjoy hurting you."

She stared at him in shocked horror. In all their years together he had never shown her this dark side of his ruthlessness.

"Are you surprised, little girl?" he asked softly, each word a blow. "Don't you know that you can goad a man just so far before he breaks?"

"Steve, please," she whispered helplessly.

"Please what?" he asked. "Please let you jump into bed with this bastard?"

"Let her go, Jason," Rex said coolly, rising to his feet. "You've frightened her enough. You don't really want to hurt her."

"Stay out of this, Brody," Steve said through his teeth. "The only thing that's saving you is that I know what kind of provocation she offered you." Steve's gaze never left her frightened face. "I know very well, don't I, Jenny?" he asked, his eyes blazing stormily. "Does it amuse you to see us roasting slowly over the flames?"

"No," Jenny gasped. "It wasn't like that. It wasn't ever meant to be like that." The tears flowed down her cheeks.

"Can't you see that she's just a kid?" Rex broke in roughly. "She didn't realize what she was doing to you."

"Don't you tell me about Jenny!" Steve snarled. "She's mine. She's always been mine." He was breathing heavily, his whole body vibrating with electricity. To Jenny's frightened eyes, he looked like a Viking warrior about to claim his plunder.

He turned suddenly and strode rapidly toward the door, dragging her along behind him.

Rex followed and grabbed Steve urgently by the arm. Steve turned with the deadly swiftness of a striking cobra, his eyes blazing furiously.

"No!" Jenny said sharply, and threw herself between them. "Leave Rex alone, Steve. This is all my fault. If you have to hit someone, let it be me."

She turned to Rex and said with shaky dignity, "I'm sorry to have involved you in this, Rex. Please forgive me."

"You don't have to go with him, mermaid," Rex said quietly, his dark eyes narrowed on her white face. "Just say the word."

Jenny shook her head. "Stay out of it, Rex," she ordered huskily. "It's my battle, not yours."

"Very wise," Steve said in a tight voice. "Shall we go while your lover is still in one piece?"

She didn't try to fight him this time when he grasped her by the elbow and pushed her ahead of him out of the suite. She followed his lead dazedly as he guided her through the corridors and into the elevator, pressing the button for the penthouse.

Nine

When they reached the apartment, Steve used his key to open the front door. "I told Mike he wouldn't be needed any more tonight," he said grimly. He closed and locked the door behind him.

Jenny whirled to face him. "Please, this has all been a mistake," she burst out, trying to see the Steve Jason she knew behind the rigid, furious mask.

"Yes, it has," he said coolly, taking off his jacket and tie. "You've never made a greater one. Go into the bedroom and wait for me."

She turned and walked slowly toward her room.

"My bedroom, Jenny," he said softly behind her.

She stopped, feeling the breath leave her body. It was replaced by such a turmoil of emotions that it made her dizzy. She turned back to him, her eyes wide with shock.

"What difference does it make whose bed you occupy tonight, mine or Brody's?" he asked, his lips curving in a bitter smile. "After all, what you want is experience, isn't it? I'm in the mood to give you all you can handle."

"Not like this. Not when you're so angry with me," she whispered, searching wildly for some sign of softening in his demeanor.

"Changed your mind? That's too bad!" he said, his face hard. "Because tonight you're going to give me everything you've been teasing me with for the last two weeks. Get into that bedroom, Jenny. I'll join you after I have a drink. If I don't calm down a little, your first 'experience' may be rape."

He turned and vanished into the living room, leaving her gazing after him helplessly. She bit her lower lip. She'd never been afraid of Steve before, but she was afraid now. She turned and walked slowly into his room and closed the door behind her. She leaned back against it in the darkness, breathing as heavily as if she'd been running. Whatever she imagined it would be like, it was not like this. Steve had looked at her as though he hated her. She rubbed her wrist where red marks were already showing on her delicate skin. He had hurt her.

She had been such a fool, she thought miserably. How could she have thought she could manipulate a man like Steve Jason? She may have wrecked any chance she might have had with him. She felt a sudden panic rise in her and she turned and wrenched open the door, thinking only of flight.

"Going somewhere?" Steve walked toward her with a menacing grace. Jenny found herself backing away from him hurriedly, into the bedroom. He closed the door behind him and leaned against it, a mocking smile on his face.

"Poor Jenny," he jeered softly. His hand touched the wall switch and the room was flooded with light. His eyes ran over her with insulting intimacy, lingering on the high curve of her breasts.

"You're very lovely," he drawled. "Even in that tart's dress." He took a step forward and grasped her by the shoulders. There was a flickering flame in the depth of his eyes. "The drink didn't help," he said huskily.

His mouth closed on her with a bruising ferocity, parting her lips to invade her with his tongue. She tried to breathe, but his lips were working hotly on hers until she was arching mindlessly to the hard curve of his body, her mouth offered in helpless subjection to the pleasure he was taking and giving.

She felt a sudden coolness as his deft hands dispensed with the zipper of her gown and pushed the material off her shoulders impatiently. She gasped and then shuddered convulsively as his hands closed on her breasts, his thumbs teasing the nipples to hard arousal. She made a sound deep in her throat that was almost a groan, but his mouth on hers muffled it. His tongue and fingers worked ceaselessly until she was as pliant as clay in his experienced hands. Her knees suddenly buckled and she sagged against him weakly.

He gave a savage, triumphant laugh and lifting her, carried her over to the king-sized bed. His hands stripped her swiftly.

Her own hands flew out instinctively to cover herself. "Please, Steve, the lights," she pleaded.

He shook his head. He took her wrists in one hand and pulled them deliberately away from her body and over her head, pinning them there. "I want to see every inch of you," he said. "I came close to ripping the clothes off you a half dozen times last week. Now I want to enjoy every teasing curve of that luscious body."

She felt the blood rush to the surface of her skin as his eyes did, indeed, study each curve and valley with a passionate intensity. He lowered his head slowly and his mouth covered a taut nipple, nipping and teasing it with his tongue and teeth, then switching to the other peak until she was sobbing with the exquisite, tormenting need he was creating.

"Steve. Please, Steve," she moaned. He released her finally, standing up to strip quickly, and then he was back with her. How beautiful he was, she thought dazedly, as he fitted his body to hers. So strong and golden. A distant memory stirred. Apollo. Then she couldn't think at all. His hands were moving, molding her, his body rubbing sensuously against her own until she was whimpering with hunger.

The blazing blue of his eyes was glazed with passion and a taut anger. How could he still feel anger, she thought wildly. How could he feel anything but this mindless desire for completion? Steve's hands were driving her insane while he took her lips in swift, biting kisses.

"You love all this, don't you, Jenny?" he murmured silkily. "I knew you'd be this responsive. You love this, don't you?" His delving hand made a motion that caused her to jerk with pleasure. "Tell me how much you love it."

"I love it," she gasped, writhing, her head thrashing from side to side on the pillow.

His hand moved again, causing her to shudder and arch against him. "You love that, too. Don't you, Jenny?"

"Yes," she panted helplessly, wondering why he was tormenting her.

His hands moved to her face, cradling it, so that she was forced to meet his steady gaze. He said softly, "If I hadn't come for you tonight, you'd be in Brody's bed, letting Brody touch you like this."

"No," she gasped, her eyes widening in shock. She tried to roll away from him.

"Yes," he said savagely, holding her immovable beneath him. "I could kill you for even thinking of letting him do this to you!"

His mouth covered hers in a suffocating kiss. Then his knee was parting her thighs and he was on top of her, holding her still as he stared down at her with hot blue eyes. He bent and kissed her, his tongue entering her intimately. Suddenly he drove into her and his lips on hers muffled her cry of pain. His mouth left hers and his voice was hoarse and wild as he plunged again and again, driving her insane with a fury of desire.

"You belong to me. You'll always belong to me. Say it!"

"I belong to you," she repeated breathlessly.

"You'll never let another man touch you," he urged fiercely. "Tell me!"

"No," she moaned. "Never!"

Then he was done with talk. He enveloped her with a towering blaze of passion. She was a salamander writhing in the flame, content to be there if he was there with her. And he was there, he was

everywhere, until she finally knew that he himself was the flame. Then suddenly she was the flame, too.

She lay against his shoulder, her breathing gradually quieting, her hand curled in the rough golden hair on his chest. His arms were holding her snugly to him and abruptly she was aware of the glaring lights. A hot blush dyed her cheeks as she looked down at her nude body. "Can't we turn out the lights now?" she whispered hesitantly.

He looked down at her, all anger gone from his eyes, and one hand reached up to trace the line of her cheekbone. "It's a shocking waste," he argued lazily, then pressed a button on the bedside table, plunging the room into darkness.

She cuddled close to him again, feeling him fumble at the bedside table. She heard the click of the cigarette lighter as he lit a cigarette. He inhaled deeply, the orange tip glowing in the darkness.

"It's no wonder you're a rake," she said suddenly.

"I beg your pardon?"

"If it's always like this, I can understand why

you're always going to bed with someone," she said earnestly. "It's surprising that you ever get out of bed at all."

"I do have a few other interests," he said, a thread of amusement in his voice.

"But this is so . . ." She broke off, searching for a word that would encompass the world shaking emotions she'd just experienced. She shrugged helplessly.

"It's all of that." He chuckled, stroking her long silky hair. He lifted her chin and gave her a warm, smokey kiss. "I'll tell you a secret that will probably make you very vain," he said gently. "It's not like this all the time. This is very, very special." He kissed her again. "You're a dynamite lady, Jenny."

"Good," she said with blissful satisfaction. "Does that mean we get to do it again?"

He crushed out his cigarette in the ashtray, then rolled her over until she was lying on top of him. "I'm glad you're so eager," he said huskily. "Because I fully intended to see that you're so exhausted you won't be able to get out of this bed in the morning."

It seemed that he meant it. He took her innumerable times that night, each time demonstrating to her again and again that he could lift her to a raging pinnacle of feeling. Jenny found herself lost in a labyrinth of passion as fiery as that first tempestuous journey, but now there was an element of tenderness added that was so exquisite, it was almost painful.

By morning she was as exhausted as he'd predicted, but still came hungrily to his arms while tears of emotion poured down her cheeks. Steve went still against her, then quietly pulled the coverlet over both of them and cradled her with infinite gentleness until she fell asleep.

His arms tightened around her soft pliant form, his gaze on the lovely high curve of her cheekbone. So beautiful and so very much his own. Now more than ever. The long battle was over and he had lost. In a few hours he would have to set his mind to thinking how to protect Jenny from the fruits of her victory, but that could wait. Now he would allow himself to just hold her in his arms and watch over his darling Jenny while she slept.

When Jenny awoke, the rays of the brilliant noonday sun were bathing the room. She came awake all at once as she usually did, and when she opened her eyes, it was with the delicious anticipation of a child on her birthday, expecting presents. She felt a momentary disappointment when she noticed the empty pillow beside her, then relaxed with a sigh of infinite contentment as Steve strode out of the bathroom dressed in a calf-length white toweling robe, his golden hair darkened from the shower.

She sat up hurriedly, pulling up the sheet and tucking it under her arms. Why did she suddenly feel so shy when last night she'd had no inhibitions at all about being naked in his arms?

"Good morning," she said breathlessly, her eyes shining like silver stars in her eager face. "It's very late, isn't it? Give me fifteen minutes to shower and I'll be right with you."

"Good morning," he answered, his blue eyes twinkling. "I believe under the circumstances a slight tardiness is understandable." He sat down beside her on the bed and cupped her face in his hands, looking down at her with such aching tenderness that it filled her with a happiness that made her dizzy. "In fact, if we didn't have quite a few things to do today, I'd be tempted to crawl back into bed and take up where we left off last night." His lips tasted hers with teasing lightness, his tongue tracing the full curve of her lower lip. "I have an idea you're going to be a constant temptation to me, love."

"Good," Jenny said, as her arms went around him, her face pressed to the springy golden mat of his chest. He smelled so good. Soap and cologne and a lovely musky male scent that was very arousing. "I think that's a wonderful idea." Her tongue darted out and stroked one of his nipples teasingly.

She felt him harden against her and he inhaled sharply. His hands slid caressingly down to her bare shoulders. "Jenny," he said huskily. "Sweet Jenny."

Then suddenly he was pushing her away, his expression taut and stern. "No, Jenny," he said. "Not now." He stood up and walked to the black velvet easy chair a few discreet yards away.

"Why not?" Jenny asked bewilderedly. "I want you to make love to me." Her eyes were cloudy with hurt. "Don't you want me, Steve?"

"Of course I want you," he said as he dropped

down into the chair and gazed at her with brooding impatience. "It's not that easy, Jenny. We've got to talk."

She brushed a lock of hair from her face, moistening her lips nervously. What could there possibly be to talk about after last night? "I don't understand," she said slowly.

"The status quo has changed," he said, not looking at her. "You got your way, Jenny. You're a married woman in every sense of the word." His glance flicked to her face and he smiled wryly. "And I might add I enjoyed every minute of initiating you into that state. I still think my way was better for all concerned, but there's no going back now. We'll just have to make the best of the situation as it now stands."

"I don't know what you're talking about," Jenny said, her eyes suddenly wide with fright.

Steve looked away again. "I mean we'll live together as man and wife, but there'll be no children," he said bluntly. "I've made an appointment for you for this afternoon at three with Dr. Eve Littleton. She has an excellent reputation and I'm sure you'll find her very understanding."

"Understanding?" Jenny asked numbly.

"She's a gynecologist," Steve said. "There will probably be a brief examination and then she'll prescribe the Pill. You'll probably be out of the office in thirty minutes."

"The Pill," she repeated dazedly. She felt as sick as if he had suggested that she take arsenic instead of a contraceptive. "Why, Steve?"

"For God's sake, you're just a baby yourself," he said roughly. "You won't want to be burdened by a child for quite a few years yet."

"Won't I?" she said, blinking rapidly to stave off the tears. "I rather thought I might. Not right away, of course, but I wasn't discounting the possibility altogether." But evidently Steve had, she thought, with a surge of almost agonizing pain. He was willing to accept her into his bed now that she'd forced the issue, but he wasn't about to permit her to bear his child. He thought she was too immature to be a full partner to him in this vitally important aspect of their relationship.

"Don't be ridiculous," Steve said briskly, as he rose to his feet. "You know I'm right about this, Jenny. Once you consider all the possible repercussions, I'm sure you'll agree with me." He strode to the bedroom door. "I think I'll go get a cup of coffee and tell Mike he'll be driving you to your appointment." He paused at the door, his hand tightening spasmodically on the door knob. "Unless you'd like me to take you?"

"No, that won't be necessary," Jenny said quietly, her lashes veiling the pain in her eyes.

The door closed quietly behind him.

Thank God he'd gone, Jenny thought desperately, as she tossed the covers aside and leaped out of bed. Another minute and she would have broken down and wailed like the baby he thought her. She ran to the closet and blindly jerked a terry cloth robe off the hanger. She slipped it on, tied the sash hurriedly, and then ran from the master suite toward the haven of her own bedroom.

"Chicken?" Mike was standing in the hall before her, a bag of groceries in his arms and a worried frown on his face.

"Not now, Mike," she said brokenly, brushing by him and slamming the door of her room behind her.

Mike gave a soundless whistle and cast a glowering glance at the door of the master suite. Then he turned and strode purposely back into the kitchen where Steve was sitting at the kitchen table, gazing gloomily down at his coffee.

"Well, you've done it this time," Mike growled, slamming the bag of groceries down on the counter by the refrigerator. "Does it give you some kind of kick to tear her to pieces? She just ran past me looking like she'd just spent a charming interlude with the Marquis de Sade."

"Shut up, Mike," Steve said.

"I don't care what she put you through," Mike said roughly, pulling the milk and eggs out of the bag. "She's just a kid, damn it. She only did it because she's crazy about you. Couldn't you have tried being a little understanding?"

"Damn it, shut up, Mike! Do you think I enjoy hurting her? It's killing me." Steve drew a deep shuddering breath, and his lips twisted as he met Mike's stunned eyes. "Did you think I was some kind of iron man? I have feelings too, you know."

"There are quite a few people who have reason to doubt that," Mike said slowly. "You're one tough customer, Steve."

"Not where Jenny's concerned," he said huskily. "You should know that by now." He made an effort at control and then looked up to say quietly, "I've made an appointment for Jenny at three with a gynecologist. You'll be driving her."

"Thanks a lot," Mike said caustically. "So that's why she looked so shaken up. Did it ever occur to you that's a very personal choice for a woman?"

"It occurred to me," Steve said, his lips curving in a bittersweet smile. "It also occurred to me that a few years from now she may discover that it wasn't love but sex that she actually felt for me. When that time comes, I'll be damned if I'll have her tied to me with bonds she'll feel are impossible to break."

Mike shook his head. "You're wrong, Steve," he said, his hazel eyes troubled. "Give her a chance. She might surprise you."

"Just be available to drive her to Dr. Littleton's office," Steve said as he stood up. "I'll be in my office if you need me for anything."

He turned and strode out of the kitchen.

TEN

JENNY WENT STRAIGHT through her bedroom to the adjoining bathroom, shedding Steve's robe carelessly on the way. She turned on the shower and ducked beneath its soothing flow. Oh God, she thought, please let me get out of here before I have to see Steve again. Why had she let herself be hurt like this? Why couldn't she have understood that sex didn't always equal love to a man of Steve's experience? She'd thought she would explode with pain as she sat and listened to Steve so coolly discuss the tidy sterile plans he had for their relationship. How had he thought that she could bear it? If she couldn't have a lifetime commitment from Steve, she'd rather have nothing at all.

She stepped out of the shower and dried herself off hurriedly. Pulling her hair over one shoulder, she quickly braided it into a single thick braid and strode purposely into the bedroom. She grabbed the first article of clothing that came to her hand when she opened the bureau drawer. It proved to be the worn faded jeans that she'd arrived in Las Vegas with. She quickly slipped on a tailored oxford blouse and stepped into a pair of brown loafers.

Casting one glance at the mirror as she pulled her ancient flight bag out of the closet, she received a small shock. She'd forgotten how young she looked in these slightly disreputable jeans. With her hair in the long childish braid, she could pass for fifteen. Then she shrugged and turned away. After all, it wasn't what was on the outside that mattered, but her own knowledge of her maturity. She was grown up, damn it, and just as capable of giving Steve what he needed as one of his sophisticated Amazons.

She quickly threw a few sets of underthings and

a pair of pajamas into the flight bag and strode briskly out of the bedroom, almost tripping over Mike, who was leaning against the wall waiting for her to emerge.

"And just where the hell do you think you're going?" he asked grimly.

"I don't have the faintest idea as yet," Jenny replied. "But you can bet it won't be to see Dr. Littleton."

Mike frowned. "Look, chicken, I know you're upset, but you know as well as I do that this is a mistake. For God's sake, stop and think what you're doing. You can't just run off half-cocked. Steve will be climbing the walls when he finds out you're gone."

"Too bad," Jenny said unsympathetically. "I'm my own person and I intend to run my own life from now on. Steve will just have to get used to it."

Mike shook his head. "That I'd like to see," he said skeptically. He tugged at her braid affectionately, then said persuasively, "At least let me call Steve and tell him what you're planning. Give the man a chance to talk to you."

Jenny shook her head. "There's nothing more to

talk about," she said bitterly. "Steve made his views quite clear."

Mike nibbled at his lip in worried exasperation. "I'm tempted to call him anyway. This is just plain crazy, Jenny!"

"No!" she said sharply. "You've got to promise me you won't tell him until after I've gone."

"I can't do that, Jenny," Mike said, hazel eyes troubled. "I owe it to Steve to let him know what you're up to, damn it! Las Vegas isn't the safest town in the world for a kid like you to be running around on your own."

Jenny realized that what she was asking was unfair to her old friend. Mike owed his loyalty first to Steve as his employer, but at the moment she couldn't afford to be fair. If Steve knew of her decision to leave, he would be a far more formidable opponent than Mike.

"You'll have to give me your promise, Mike," Jenny said with uncharacteristic ruthlessness, "because if you don't, I won't give you mine."

"And what promise is that?" Mike asked warily.

"My promise to call you and let you know where I am once I'm permanently settled."

He gave a silent whistle. "That's a low blow, chicken," he said gruffly. "You know I'll go nuts worrying about you."

She flushed, but stuck firmly to her resolve. "Is it a deal?"

He shrugged. "I have no choice, do I? Of course I won't call Steve."

She breathed a sigh of relief. "Thank you, Mike," she said and stood on tiptoe to brush a kiss on the craggy plane of his cheek. "I'll be in touch," she swore, then she hurried out of the apartment and down the elevator, her throat aching with the tears she refused to acknowledge.

Her gray eyes were still suspiciously bright as she crossed the lobby and walked out the front entrance into the stifling heat of the Las Vegas afternoon. The doorman was opening a car door for a large, obese gentleman wearing a ten gallon hat, so she walked briskly over to the row of taxis on the far side of the parking lot. She opened the door and slipped into the backseat of the first one that she came to. She vaguely noticed it was an independent cab with Dancer Taxi Service inscribed in red letters on the side.

"Where will it be, lady?" the driver asked, his gravelly voice cheerful. He turned around to look at her and grinned genially. His bright, youthful blue eyes belied the age declared by his lined face and grizzled gray hair. "It's sure hot today, isn't it?"

Jenny nodded. "Yes, it is," she replied absently. Where was she going to go, she wondered. She'd been so hurt and angry she hadn't thought beyond that panicky urge for flight. Now she was faced with all the practicalities. "I haven't decided," she said faintly. "Couldn't we just drive around for a while?"

The driver shrugged. "It's your money, lady," he said, flipping up the arm of the meter. He started the motor and pulled swiftly into the street.

Money. The word hit her with the force of a blow. She would need money. It was something she'd not had to worry about before. There had always been Steve to shelter and care for her since that first meeting on Santa Flores. Well, she could no longer rely on Steve and she most certainly would not run up bills to his account. She had enough cash in her personal checking account to last her for some time, but she'd be damned if she'd use it unless absolutely necessary.

"Something wrong, lady?" The taxi driver had been observing her worried frown through the rear view mirror. He'd been curious about the kid ever since she'd hopped into his cab. He'd thought then that she was a peculiar patron for the very expensive Santa Flores, in her shabby jeans and casual shirt. Well, all the kids today seemed to live in that particular uniform. Her daddy could probably buy and sell Charlie Dancer Incorporated.

Jenny looked up hopefully, her face brightening. Weren't taxi drivers supposed to know something about the towns they cruised? And this one had kind eyes and the nicest smile, she noticed with relief. Her gaze flew to his identification badge on the meter. Charles Dancer.

"Mr. Dancer, I wonder if you could give me some advice?" she asked quickly. "I need a place to stay tonight and I don't have much money. Could you recommend an inexpensive motel?"

"How inexpensive?" he asked flatly.

She calculated swiftly. She probably would have to count on two nights at a motel as well as meals.

She must be very careful since she intended to pay Steve back every penny. "I couldn't afford more than fifteen dollars a night."

Charlie Dancer groaned mentally. Fifteen dollars for a motel room in Las Vegas?

Jenny read the answer in his face. "Is it that hopeless?"

"I know of one place," Dancer said, his blue eyes hesitant. "But you wouldn't want to stay there."

"If it's cheap, I would," Jenny said firmly. "I don't care what it's like as long as it has a bed."

"Oh, it has a bed all right," Dancer said wryly. "Look, it's not a place for a kid like you. Don't you have any friends you could stay with? Where are your parents?"

"My parents are dead," Jenny said, frowning. "And I have no one in Las Vegas I can go to." Then she smiled into his worried face. She'd been right in thinking Charles Dancer was a very nice man. "I'll be fine. Would you tell me the name of the motel, please?"

Dancer sighed resignedly. "I'll take you there."

The motel was on the outskirts of town, a U-shaped one-story structure of red brick. It didn't look nearly as bad as the taxi driver had hinted, Jenny thought with relief. The courtyard was clean and the units seemed to be in good repair. The only really distasteful thing about it was the unbearably cute name emblazoned in bold neon script on the sign in front, 'DEW DROP INN.'

"Dew Drop Inn," Jenny echoed thoughtfully.

Dancer's eyes flew swiftly to the rear view mirror. "You've heard of it?" he asked.

She shook her head. "I was just thinking what a ghastly name it has," she said, making a face.

"In more ways than one," Dancer murmured obscurely.

"It seems to be a very popular place." There were cars parked in front of almost every unit. "Perhaps there won't be a vacancy," Jenny said, frowning worriedly.

"They'll have a vacancy," Dancer said with certainty, as he swung the taxi into the motel courtyard. "If they're occupied right now, you can come with me to lunch and I'll drop you off on the way back. There's sure to be an opening by then."

They halted in front of the glass enclosed office and he turned to face her. "You'd better give me your fifteen dollars and let me go in and reserve a room for you. The manager here doesn't like to rent to youngsters like you."

Jenny obediently gave him the money, her face puzzled. What earthly difference did it make how old she was? Dancer was out of the cab and into the office before she had a chance to ask him.

He came out a few minutes later with a key in his hand and got back into the taxi. "Got it," he said briefly. "Number twenty-nine." He started the car and drove with amazing familiarity to the far end of the court to park before a unit with a large brass twenty-nine on the door.

Dancer was out of the cab and around to the passenger side with spry swiftness. He opened the door and took her flight bag from her. As she started to open her purse, he put up his hand. "Forget it," he said gruffly. "Mail it to me when you're flush, kid."

She shook her head determinedly. She was not going to start her new life by accepting charity. "You've been too generous already," she said, placing the money into his reluctant hand. "I appreciate your help, Mr. Dancer."

He shook his head ruefully, then carried her bag to the door and unlocked it deftly. He opened it and looked around quickly before turning back to her with a relieved expression on his face. He handed her the key. "This isn't the classiest joint in town," Dancer said awkwardly. "You'd be wise to keep your door locked at all times."

She nodded with a smile, touched by his concern. "I will," she promised. "Thank you again, Mr. Dancer."

He still stood there, a troubled expression on his face. "You should be all right for one night," he said uneasily. "Just don't open your door without making sure who's on the other side."

"I'll be careful," she replied solemnly, trying to hide a smile as she took her flight bag from him. Her youthful appearance quite often brought out the protectiveness in people, but Dancer's concern seemed a bit out of proportion.

Dancer took a business card out of his jacket pocket and handed it to her. "If you run into any trouble, call me."

"That's very kind of you, Mr. Dancer," she said, smiling warmly. "But I hope it won't be necessary."

"Me too," he muttered beneath his breath as he turned away. "You just do what I said and you should be okay." He touched his hand to his cap and climbed back into the cab. He started the engine, but waited until she'd entered the room and closed the door before he backed out of the parking space.

Inside, Jenny gazed around in amazement. The tiny room contained the most enormous bed she'd ever seen in her entire life. In fact, the room was almost wall-to-wall bed. There were no chairs, no bureau, just the huge bed and one nightstand crammed into one corner. Oh yes, there was a wall-mounted shelf opposite the bed that held a portable TV and a video cassette recorder with a stack of video tapes beside it. Whoever had decorated the room had evidently tried to create the illusion of spaciousness, she thought, for there were mirrors everywhere. The far wall was entirely mirrored and there was a large framed mirror by the bathroom door. Even the ceiling was mirrored, she saw incredulously. She wondered briefly why they'd just not thought to put a smaller bed in the room. It would have accomplished the same purpose.

She threw her flight bag on the red taffeta bed-spread and edged around the bed to a black telephone on the nightstand. She perched gingerly on the monstrous bed while she searched through her handbag for her address book.

On the drive to the motel she'd tried to think of her alternatives. The sudden realization of her helpless position, thanks to her poverty, had shaken her. It was all very well to make a grand gesture and march out of Steve's life until it came time to pay the piper. She had grudgingly come to the conclusion that she must get advice and help despite her reluctance to do so.

She couldn't go to Mike. She'd already taken advantage of his friendship and loyalty to force him to do something that was contrary to his ethics. That left only one person in Las Vegas that she looked upon as a close enough friend to go to in time of need. She quickly dialed the number of Rex Brody's suite at the Santa Flores.

The phone rang for quite a long time before it was answered by an extremely irritable Rex.

"Hello," he barked.

"Rex?" Jenny said nervously. "This is Jenny Jason."

"I should have known," Rex said resignedly. "Who else would let the damn phone ring off the hook?"

"I'm sorry," she said in a small voice. "Were you in the shower or something?"

"Or something," he said succinctly. Suddenly he uttered a surprised "Ouch!" and there was a distinctly feminine giggle in the background. "I'm pretty busy at the moment, Jenny," he said. "Could I call you back?"

Jenny could feel the color flood her face and she was glad that Rex wasn't there to tease her about her naivete. "Certainly," she stammered. "I'm sorry I disturbed you."

"Forget it. Shall I call you back at your apartment?"

"No," she said. "I'll give you the number." She reached for a book of matches on the nightstand and read the number off the cover quickly. "It's the Dew Drop Inn," she ended. "Did you get the number?"

"Got it," he said briskly. "I'll call—" Abruptly he

broke off and there was a puzzling silence. Then Rex asked carefully, "Where did you say you were calling from?"

"The Dew Drop Inn," Jenny said. "It's a motel. I've taken a room here."

There was another long silence. "Would it be too much to ask why you've taken a room at the Dew Drop Inn?" he asked politely.

"It's a long story and you're busy," she said hurriedly. "I apologize for having bothered you. Goodbye, Rex."

"Jenny!" he roared. "Are you still there?"

"Yes, I'm still here," she said, holding the phone away from her abused ear. "But it's obvious you have someone with you. I'll be glad to have you return my call, Rex."

"No, it's okay," he said. "I'm not busy."

"Are you sure?" she asked doubtfully.

"Damn it, Jenny, I told you that she's not important!" Rex growled in exasperation.

Jenny heard an indignant shriek from Rex's female companion and then a moment later the slam of a door.

She smothered a smile as Rex said glumly, "I'm

now entirely at your disposal, mermaid. What the hell is happening?"

"I've left Steve," Jenny said quietly, and just uttering the simple words sent an ache through her. "I need your advice, Rex. Would you meet me somewhere?"

There was a long pause before he replied. "So it didn't work out after all. I was afraid there wouldn't be any easy victory with a man like your husband." His voice was gentle as he said simply, "I'm sorry, Jenny."

"Me, too," she said in a throaty voice, feeling those maddening tears rush again to her eyes. She wouldn't cry, damn it! She squared her shoulders and continued brightly. "Well, now I'm on my own and I have to earn some money and find work. Will you help me?"

"Of course," Rex said absently, his mind obviously on something else. "But what the hell are you doing at that motel?"

"I had to have a place to stay," she answered reasonably. "Charles Dancer brought me here."

"Who is Charles Dancer?"

"He drives a cab," Jenny explained. "He was very kind to me."

"I just bet he was."

"I'm very grateful to him," Jenny said defensively. "It's not at all a bad place, though it's decorated rather strangely. Do you know what's on the ceiling?"

"Mirrors," Rex stated flatly.

"How did you know?" Jenny asked in amazement. "Have you stayed here before?"

"No, I haven't been there before," he grated. "Stay right where you are. I'll get dressed and be right over."

Suddenly the idea of staying cooped up in this tiny mirrored box until Rex arrived was repugnant to her. "I haven't had lunch yet," she said restlessly. "I noticed a diner just down the street. Could we meet there?"

"No! Stay in your room. I'll bring you something."

"All right. I suppose I'll watch TV until you get here." She eyed the TV and cassette player with casual speculation. "Or maybe I'll watch a movie.

There seem to be quite a few video tapes to choose from."

"No! Don't do that!" Rex said so sharply it startled her. She heard him draw a deep breath and then he said more calmly, "Look, Jenny, why don't you just take a little nap until I get there? I won't be more than thirty minutes."

"Very well." She sighed resignedly. "I'm in room twenty-nine."

"Right," he said curtly. "Now don't open that door until I get there!" The dial tone sounded abruptly as Rex hung up.

Jenny replaced the receiver, shaking her head in exasperation. Rex was being as overprotective as Charles Dancer. Why was it that all the men in her life persisted in thinking of her as a helpless doll unable to function in the real world?

Jenny didn't have long to wait. There was a knock on the door five minutes earlier than Rex's promised thirty minutes. When she opened the door with an eager smile, she was confronted by dark, worried eyes and a displeased scowl. Rex was dressed in light gray slacks and a navy short sleeved sport shirt, and his crisp dark hair seemed to be damp from a hurried shower.

"You didn't even ask who it was before opening the door," he growled, as he pushed past her into the room and handed her a bag with a familiar golden arch imprinted on it. "A Big Mac, fries, and a soda," he said. "I didn't want to take time for anything in the gourmet line."

"This will be fine," Jenny said cheerfully. She waved a hand casually. "You'll have to sit on the bed, there don't seem to be any chairs." She kicked off her shoes and crawled to the center of the bed. She settled herself tailor fashion and eagerly opened the bag and extracted the food. She spread her feast on several of the paper napkins that were in the bag. Only then did she look up and see Rex still standing in the same spot, exasperation and amusement conflicting on his dark face.

"Would you like a french fry?" Jenny offered politely.

Amusement won, and Rex shook his head ruefully. "You're incredible, do you know that?" He sat gingerly on the bed and leaned over to take one of the french fries. "I rush over here to rescue a maiden in distress and just look at you. You're a great disappointment to me, mermaid."

"Sorry about that," Jenny said serenely. "I may be heartbroken, but I learned a long time ago the only way to survive unhappiness was to live one moment at a time."

Brody shot her a keen glance. "That's an amazingly streetwise bit of knowledge for a girl as sheltered as you've been."

Jenny smiled sadly as she recalled how very different her life had been than Rex's imaginings. There had been nothing sheltered about her existence before Steve had stepped in and taken charge. Now she would once again have to face up to the loneliness and insecurity without that beloved presence.

"I need a job, Rex, and a place to stay. I thought I might get work as a governess or domestic until I get on my feet. Do you suppose you could recommend me to one of your friends?" she asked.

Rex shook his head wryly. "My friends aren't the sort that keep the home fires burning, and there's no way I'd send a wide-eyed lamb like you into their lecherous clutches." He took another french fry. "Don't worry, I'll find something for you."

"You'll have to move fast," Jenny said, making a face. "I can't afford to stay here more than two nights."

A swift frown crossed Rex's face. "You're not staying here for even one night," he said. "As soon as you finish that hamburger, I'm taking you to another motel."

"No, you're not. I can't afford to stay anywhere else," Jenny said stubbornly. "This motel may not be five star, but it's quite inexpensive."

"I imagine it is," Rex said dryly. "They sometimes rent the same room ten or twelve times a night."

"What?" Jenny asked blankly, staring at him as if he'd lost his mind.

"Jenny, you've either got to be the most innocent woman alive or the stupidest. Look around you, for God's sake. Mirrors on the ceiling, a wall-to-wall bed, and I'll wager those cassettes are all pornographic."

Jenny's eyes widened. "You mean . . ."

"I mean, my dreamy-eyed friend, that you managed to rent yourself a room in a motel that's notorious for being frequented by every freelance call girl and prostitute in Las Vegas," Rex said. "The place is always being raided for one reason or another." He ran his fingers through his dark hair. "Now will you please finish eating so I can get you out of here?"

Jenny took another bite of her sandwich, her face thoughtful. "So that's why Mr. Dancer was worried."

"What? Oh, you mean your cab driver friend?" he asked grimly. "I just wonder what plans he had in mind for you."

"He was a very nice man," Jenny said indignantly. "For goodness sake, he's old enough to be my grandfather!"

"Even you must have heard of dirty old men," Rex said. "Kindly grandfather types don't usually bring pretty young girls to places like the Dew Drop Inn. If you ask me, he was thinking of paying you a visit later tonight."

Jenny bolted upright. "He was not! Rex Brody, that's a terribly cynical thing to say."

"I'm a terribly cynical man, Jenny," Rex said

wearily. "And you're a babe in the woods." He watched her consume the last of her meal with barely concealed impatience. "Now may we get out of here?" he asked, as she put the wrappers, cup, and napkins in the sack.

"I'm not going anywhere," Jenny said coolly. "This place is the only one I can afford and nothing you've said has changed that fact." She put the sack on the bedside table. "I won't feel hurt if you want to leave, however. If I were picked up in a raid, no one would care. But Rex Brody caught in a vice den would be pretty sensational publicity."

"It would probably make me more popular than ever," Rex said cynically. "But I can guarantee Steve Jason would care quite a bit if his wife was picked up by the police."

Jenny hadn't thought of that. She shivered involuntarily at the thought of exactly how displeased Steve would be if that occurred. Then she shrugged. "It doesn't concern him any longer," she said with false bravado. "Besides, what are the odds of there being a raid on the particular nights that I'm here?"

"Judging by your past record, about ninety-nine to one against you." Rex bit his lip. "You know that money's not a problem," he said gruffly. "I can let you have whatever you need. If you won't accept it any other way, consider it a loan."

"Thanks, Rex," Jenny said softly, her silver eyes glowing with gratitude. "I can't accept your money, but I will accept your help. If you want me out of this den of iniquity, you'll just have to find me a job."

"Damn it, Jenny, you know that I can't just walk out and leave you here."

"There's a lock on the door," Jenny pointed out cheerfully. "I'll be perfectly safe."

A sharp knock sounded on the door, startling both of them.

Jenny made a motion to answer it, but Rex stopped her with an impatient frown. "Locks don't do much good when you open the door to anybody who knocks," he said caustically. "Ask who's there, for God's sake!"

Jenny smiled sheepishly and obediently called out. "Who's there?"

"Charlie Dancer."

"What did I tell you?" Rex exploded, his black eyes flashing. "Some grandfather!" He rose to his feet. "Well, I have a few words to say to Mr. Charlie Dancer."

Jenny frowned. "Rex! No! I'm sure it's perfectly . . ."

But Rex had already thrown open the door, belligerence in every line of his body. It was met by an answering antagonism as Charles Dancer's keen appraisal took in both Rex and, beyond him, Jenny on her knees in the middle of the bed.

Dancer attacked first. "Who the hell are you?" he asked roughly. He looked back at Jenny. "I told you not to open the door. It's a good thing I came back." He pushed Rex aside and entered the room. "It's not been two hours and you've got this flashy young stud nosing around you."

Surprise and indignation tempered the belligerence on Rex's face. "I'm not nosing around her," he said defensively, then added more aggressively, "And what are you doing creeping around her like some aging pervert?"

"Rex, he's no such thing," Jenny said quickly.

"Pervert?" Dancer said, his cheeks ruddy with anger. "Now, listen here—"

"No, you listen!" Rex interrupted, jabbing a finger at Dancer's chest. "Who but a lousy pervert would bring Jenny to a place like this?"

Jenny's lips tightened. "Rex, that's going too far," she said sternly.

"No, he's right," Dancer said awkwardly. "I knew this was no place for a kid like you. That's why I came back. I called my wife, Lottie, and we talked it over. She wants me to bring you home with me tonight."

Jenny shot a triumphant glance at Rex's stunned face, but refrained from uttering the gleeful, I-told-you-so that was trembling on her tongue. "That's wonderful of you both, Mr. Dancer, but I can't take advantage of your generosity," she said warmly.

"Oh no, she wouldn't think about jeopardizing her precious independence by accepting a little help," Rex said sarcastically. "She'd rather stay in this glorified bordello."

Jenny was amused to note that Rex and Mr. Dancer's antagonism had subtly shifted from each other to her. Instead of two knight errants vying to rescue her, she was confronted with a duo of very irate and indignant males united in their exasperation at what they believed to be her foolish feminine stubbornness.

"Mr. Dancer, may I present Mr. Brody. You two should get along exceptionally well," Jenny said dryly. "You have so much in common."

They both ignored this caustic introduction and began to speak.

"Jenny, you can't—"

"Miss, it's just not safe—"

The door that had been left ajar was suddenly thrown open, striking Rex in the back. He turned to face the new arrival with a curse, and his eyes widened with shocked dismay as he faced the truly intimidating bulk of Mike Novacek.

"Mike, what are you doing here?" Jenny asked in amazement.

Rex breathed a sigh of profound relief. "You know him?" he asked. "Thank God! I was afraid I was going to have to fight him."

Mike glared at him ferociously. "You still might," he growled. "You're Brody, aren't you?" He waved a massive hand that managed to indicate both the motel room and the situation. "Was this your idea?"

"Mike, will you please answer me?" Jenny asked, then frowned at him. "You gave me your word."

"I promised you I wouldn't tell Steve," Mike replied. "And I didn't, damn it. But there was no way I could let you just walk out into the steets without knowing where you were going. I called down to security and one of the men followed you when you left the hotel." He gave Brody another intimidating scowl. "It's a good thing I did, too. Do you know what kind of place this bastard has brought you to?"

"You must be Mike Novacek," Rex guessed. "You sound different on the phone," he added with a gloomy sigh. "Smaller."

"Rex didn't bring me here, Mike," Jenny explained patiently. "It was Mr. Dancer, here, and it was all—"

Mike turned suddenly to the older man, whose tanned face was suddenly a shade paler. "You brought her here?" Mike asked softly.

"Mike, stop frightening the man," Jenny said severely. "He was only doing his job."

Mike snorted. "Some job you've got, bozo, picking up nice young kids and bringing them to a motel like this." His eyes narrowed dangerously.

"He's a taxi driver, and I asked him to bring me here," Jenny said quickly. This was taking on all the aspects of a farce, she thought wildly. "I wish you'd just leave. This isn't your affair, Mike."

"It will be very much my affair if Steve finds out I knew you were leaving and didn't tell him," Mike said flatly. "He'll murder me."

"Who's Steve?" Charles Dancer croaked, wondering what manner of man could intimidate even the enormous brute facing him.

"My husband," Jenny answered absently and Dancer made a sound somewhere between a gasp and a groan.

"I'm taking you home, Jenny," Mike announced. "I should never have let you leave in the first place."

"You had no choice then and you still don't," Jenny replied, her silver eyes flashing. "You can't force me to leave here."

"I was afraid you'd say something like that," Rex groaned. "Does that mean I have to try to stop him if he decides to make the attempt?"

"Don't be ridiculous," Jenny said crossly. "Mike's not going to cause trouble."

All three men looked at her with frank skepticism.

"I'm glad you're so confident," Rex said dryly. "I seem to remember another time when you offered me similar assurances."

She opened her mouth to protest this low blow when there was a preemptory knock on the door.

Jenny closed her eyes. "This can't be happening," she murmured. "If we get one more person in this room, it will resemble a Marx Brothers movie." She opened her eyes and called resignedly, "Who is it?"

"Bill Garston," came the aggressive reply. "Let me in!"

"Who's Bill Garston?" Jenny asked blankly.

"He's the motel manager," Charles Dancer offered, rousing himself from the dazed apathy that had followed Mike's arrival.

Jenny gestured toward the door. "Let him in," she said, then added with a fatalistic sigh, "And why even bother closing the door?"

Dancer opened the door to reveal a short, dapper

man in his early fifties dressed in dark trousers and a pale pink shirt. His sharp, thin face was angry, as he asked suspiciously, "What's going on here? I've seen three guys walk through that door in the past thirty minutes. I don't give the girls any trouble if they want to bring their johns here, but I don't allow group stuff. It's too damn rough on the furniture."

"For furniture, read bed," Rex murmured, tongue-in-cheek.

Garston gave him a sharp glance and in the process his gaze encountered Jenny still kneeling in the center of the bed. His horrified eyes wandered over her slight figure, shabby blue jeans, and the childish braid falling over one shoulder.

"Jail bait," he muttered dazedly. "She can't be a day over sixteen." His eyes were snapping with anger as he turned back to Dancer. "What are you trying to do to me?" he roared. "The D.A. would just love to nab me on a morals charge, and you bring me this teenage Lolita with *two* johns!" He was almost frothing at the mouth. "Get her out of here. Do you hear me? I want her *out!*"

Jenny lifted her chin defiantly. "I'm not a Lolita!

And you have no right to throw me out when I've done absolutely nothing wrong."

Garston's face turned an apoplectic scarlet, his Adam's apple bobbing like a turkey's as he struggled to speak. "Listen, girlie, I run this motel. If I say you get out, you go!"

Jenny could feel her anger mounting by the second. Today she'd been hurt, rejected, browbeaten by all and sundry, and now this ferret-faced weasel was insulting her! "If you want to evict me, you'll have to get the police," she said hotly, her gray eyes flashing. "We'll just see who they'll believe, Mr. Garston!"

"The police!" Garston's eyes narrowed suspiciously. "My God, it's a lousy set-up! Somebody paid you to set me up, didn't they?"

"I don't know what you're talking about," Jenny said, lifting her chin even higher.

"Don't give me that," Garston snarled. "Who was it? Correllini?"

Jenny shook her head in confusion. "No," she said. "I don't—"

Garston interrupted. "It doesn't matter who it was," he rasped. "However much they paid you,

I'll double it. All you have to do is be out of this room in five minutes and I'll lay five C notes on you. Is that enough, damn it?"

Jenny's face was dazed. The man was mad. The whole world was mad. "No, I don't want—" she started.

"Seven hundred and fifty, and that's my last offer," Garston interrupted again.

"The chick won't take no less than two big ones," Rex grated suddenly in a passable Bogart voice.

Jenny stared at him, open mouthed.

Rex's dark eyes were dancing as he straightened his shoulders in a Cagney-like shrug. "You're not dealing with kids, you know," he added.

Garston's eyes darted to Rex. "Who are you? I ain't talking to no bloody pi—"

"Manager," Rex substituted smoothly.

"Rex, will you stop this," Jenny said in exasperation. "The man thinks you're serious."

Rex dropped down on the bed, his tough guy pose dissolving as he bent over double laughing.

"This is not funny," Jenny said indignantly, glaring sternly at his convulsed body and streaming eyes.

"Oh, but it is," Rex gasped, wiping his eyes. "This must be the first time in the history of the Dew Drop Inn that a girl has been paid *not* to go to bed!"

There was a sudden reluctant chuckle from Mike. Even Charles Dancer's lips were twitching uncontrollably, Jenny noted in exasperation. It was all too much.

Garston was staring at them all with violent displeasure. "Very funny!" he snarled. "I want this kid out of here. Now, who do I deal with, damn it?"

"You deal with me," Steve Jason said coolly as he plucked Garston easily out of his way and entered the room.

She supposed she should have expected it, Jenny thought despairingly. Why shouldn't Steve be here? Everybody else was.

In a dark business suit and discreet gray tie, Steve should have looked elegantly conservative, but he didn't. There was an air of restrained savagery about him, and he dominated the tiny crowded room with effortless ease, his icy blue eyes appraising his surroundings with ruthless composure.

"Hello, Jenny," he said softly, his gaze raking over her. "I see you've managed to raise yourself a little hell." Then he turned to Mike and his lips tightened ominously. "There had better be a damn good reason for you not reporting this imbroglio of Jenny's, Mike."

"I thought there was at the time," Mike said with a grimace. "I'm not so sure now. I suppose the security man went scurrying to you right after he gave me his report?"

"He evidently values his job more than you do," Steve said, and Mike flinched at the implacable toughness in his employer's face.

Jenny felt a thrill of uneasiness. She'd never heard Steve speak to Mike like that before. Had her actions really endangered Mike's livelihood?

"None of this was Mike's fault," she said defensively.

Steve's face retained its inflexible hardness as his gaze returned to her. "I'm well aware where the blame lies," he said. "And I assure you that we'll be discussing it in depth quite soon. At the moment, all I'm interested in is getting you out of here." His gaze drifted to Rex, sitting on the bed next to her, and for a moment there was a break in his iron control as his electric blue eyes flamed with rage.

Rex shook his head ruefully as he recognized how close Jason was to releasing that rage. "You'll forgive me if I don't get up, Jason," he said with a wry grimace. "This mattress will be a much better cushion than the floor."

"You're in no danger at the moment," Steve said reluctantly, gazing almost hungrily at Rex's face as if mentally choosing the points for mutilation. "I'll attend to you later."

"I'm sure you will," Rex agreed gloomily.

Steve's gaze went on to Charles Dancer, who was staring at him in bemused fascination. "You're Steve Jason," he said slowly. "You own the Santa Flores." He darted a quick glance at Jenny. Who would have believed this fresh faced kid would belong to such a powerful and dangerous man as Steve Jason?

"And who are you?" Steve asked, his eyes narrowing.

"He's just a cab driver," Jenny said hurriedly.

Poor Mr. Dancer had been through enough intimidation with Mike and Rex without exposing him to the more lethal fire of Steve Jason. "Thank you for returning my bag, Mr. Dancer," she said meaningfully. "Perhaps you'd better leave now."

"That's okay," Dancer said with relief. "Goodbye, Mrs. Jason." He touched his hand to his cap as he edged past Steve. "Mr. Jason." Then he was gone.

"You really shouldn't try to lie, Jenny," Steve said silkily. "You never learned how to do it properly. Mr. Dancer, too, will figure in our little discussion."

Bill Garston, who'd been watching Jason's assumption of command of the situation, had leaped eagerly on the only statement of interest to him. "You're taking the chick away?" he questioned eagerly, as he pushed closer and grabbed Steve by the arm. Then he gnawed his lip in anxiety. "What if she won't go?"

Steve removed Garston's hand from his arm with patent distaste. "You're the manager of this establishment?" he asked contemptuously. Garston nodded, and then flushed as Steve continued to fix him with a look of disdain. "She'll go. And after she's gone, you'll forget you've ever seen her. Do you understand?"

"Sure," Garston said, moistening his lips and backing away from the deadly menace in those icy blue eyes. "Sure. I never saw her. I never saw any of you."

"Good!" Steve said grimly. "Now get out of here!" He didn't even bother to watch as the man bolted from the room.

"You're very sure of yourself," Jenny said defiantly, her silver eyes sparking. "Why should I go to all the bother of leaving you, only to come running back when you snap your fingers?"

"I'm sure of you, Jenny," Steve said coolly. "You're very soft hearted, as I have reason to know. You couldn't take your freedom at someone else's expense." His casual glance went from Mike to Rex meaningfully. "So you'll be good and come along with me, won't you?"

Jenny's hands clenched into fists. She knew she was beaten. Steve was dangerously close to losing control. She couldn't run the risk of his venting that savage ruthlessness on two innocent men who'd only wanted to help her.

"Yes, I'll come along with you," she said, lifting her chin proudly. She added defiantly, "For now."

Steve smiled mirthlessly. "I thought you would." He turned to Mike. "I'll have a word to say to you later, Mike. I'll see you back at the apartment." It was clearly a dismissal. Mike shrugged and with a tiny grimace at Jenny, he, too, left the room.

Steve held out his hand commandingly. "Jenny?" he said arrogantly, and Jenny found herself meekly putting her hand in his. He pulled her across the bed, then placing his hands on her waist, lifted her swiftly to the floor. She felt a shock of sensation go through her at his touch, and she could see by the sudden jerk of a muscle in his cheek that he was not unaffected. She turned to Rex, who was rising slowly to his feet, his dark eyes curiously thoughtful as they went from Steve's tense face to Jenny's.

"Thanks for everything, Rex," Jenny said quietly. "I'll be in touch."

Rex shook his head ruefully. "It says quite a bit for my fondness for you, mermaid, that your promise actually fills me with pleasure and not sheer unadulterated terror." He waved a hand mockingly. "Good luck, Jenny."

She had no opportunity to answer. With a firm hand under her elbow, Steve drew her inexorably from the motel room.

ELEVEN

To Jenny's surprise, Steve didn't attempt to start their discussion once they had reached the car. He maintained a rigid, smoldering silence for the fifteen minute drive back to the Santa Flores, and it wasn't until they had arrived at the apartment that he spoke. "Go into the living room and wait for me," he said tersely, as he shut the front door. "I want to have a few words with Mike." He turned and strode swiftly to the kitchen.

It was only a scant five minutes before Steve returned. He strode into the room with the lithe hungry grace of a puma who had tasted first blood and was ready to devour his kill. Completely ignoring

Jenny, who sat in one of the chairs, he made for the bar and leisurely fixed himself a drink. As she watched him, a growing resentment was slowly building in her. Was this silent treatment supposed to intimidate her, work on her nerves so that she was softened and malleable enough to manipulate when he finally chose to give her his attention?

Steve turned to her at last, his gaze going over her sardonically. "I can see how that motel manager could mistake you for a minor. You look like a TV commercial for a runaway hotline."

She ignored the stinging condemnation in his tone and looked up at him coolly. "But I didn't run, I walked away from you, Steve. I knew exactly what I was doing when I walked out that door."

"Did you?" he asked, as he strolled from behind the bar to lean indolently against a stool. "I didn't get that impression when I found you in that extremely disreputable motel."

"Don't patronize me, Steve," Jenny said in a tired voice. "I'm sure Mike told you what happened at the motel. I won't be treated like a half-wit child for something that wasn't my fault."

"It never seems to be your fault," Steve said, his

lips thinning. "Yet you manage to end up in hot water with amazing frequency. How do you account for that?"

"I don't account for it," she said clearly. "Not to you, Steve. Not any more."

A swift frown clouded his face. Storm clouds over Mount Olympus, she thought with a curious remoteness. She wondered why she didn't feel the familiar anxiety and wretched unhappiness that always accompanied any contretemps with Steve. Then she realized it didn't matter. Nothing could be worse than what had already happened.

"Watch it, Jenny," Steve said softly, his eyes flickering like blue flames. "I've had to exercise a good deal of restraint in the last few hours. I guarantee you wouldn't enjoy it if I lost control."

Jenny rose slowly to her feet and faced him boldly. "I've been exercising quite a lot of restraint myself today," she said shakily. "I've been told to run along back to the nursery and play with my toys by my husband. I've been accused of being a prostitute by that dirty little procurer, and my 'friends' have been prodding and ordering me about as though I were nine instead of nineteen."

She drew a deep breath. "And now you have the supreme gall to treat me as if I was some retarded simpleton because of that idiotic scene at the motel. So I made the mistake of renting a room in a sleazy motel!" She ignored the sardonic arch of his eyebrow at this gross understatement. "Did it ever occur to any of you strong, wise, adult males that perhaps nothing would have happened if you'd just let me alone to run my own life as I see fit? Why must you all assume that I'm just a helpless idiot? I may lack experience, but I'm reasonably intelligent, for heaven's sake!"

She paused for breath, and for a brief instant she was sure she saw a flicker of admiration mixed with the anger in Steve's eyes. Then it was gone and Steve said coldly, "If you're quite finished, I suggest that you start at the beginning and tell me why you ran away."

She stared at him in disbelief. "Haven't you heard anything I've just said?" she asked wonderingly, then without waiting for an answer, she whirled on her heel and strode angrily toward her room.

Steve muttered a curse and called sternly, "Jenny!

Come back here. You're not leaving until we've finished talking."

"The hell I'm not!" Jenny tossed over her shoulder. "I submitted to your far-from-subtle blackmail to get me back here, but I have no intention of sitting here and being interrogated like a recalcitrant schoolgirl. I fully intend to talk to you, but it will be at a time that *I* wish." She opened the door of her room. "And that time is not now! Go back to your office, Steve. I'll come down when I'm ready." The door slammed behind her with a resounding bang.

She collapsed against the door, half expecting Steve to march after her. It was the first time in her life she could ever remember raising her voice to him. The fury that had buoyed her spirits had gone as quickly as it had come, and she felt a cold knot of misery tighten in her throat. The tears that had been threatening all day suddenly rained down her cheeks in a silent stream. She couldn't regret any of the things she'd said to Steve, but she did regret the anger and bitterness that had run through the words like a poisonous stream. It wasn't his fault he couldn't love her as she loved him. He couldn't see her as anything but the child she'd been so many years ago on Santa Flores.

She took a long time dressing and preparing herself physically and mentally for the interview. She must have time to steel herself so that she could be as cool and damnably "mature" as he was. She wore more makeup than usual and piled her hair on top of her head in a sleek bun, letting a few wispy tendrils curl about her face alluringly. She chose a sleeveless, highnecked cream sheath. Then she slipped on high heeled alligator pumps and sprayed herself generously with Shalimar.

Her lips curved in a bittersweet smile as she gazed at her reflection. Why hadn't she realized it was happening? She'd wanted so badly to regain that maturity and serene strength so that she could meet Steve on his own level. Now it was all there in the face of the woman in the mirror. Perhaps it had been the flames of passion or the agony of pain that had caused this final Renaissance. She turned away from the mirror with a weary shrug. None of it mattered now any way.

When she entered the office area, Pat Marchant looked up with a cheerful smile. "Hello, Jenny."

"Hello, Pat. I'd like to see Steve, please," Jenny announced briefly.

"Go right in," Pat said promptly. "He's expecting you."

Jenny gave the older woman a sad little smile. "I'm quite sure he is."

Steve looked up from the papers he'd been scanning. "I see you've finally deigned to honor me with your presence."

"I won't keep you long," she replied. "But I thought we should discuss arrangements before I left."

Steve's gaze ran over the chic sophistication of her ensemble with a cool appraisal that wasn't without a certain wariness. "Very nice," he commented. "Presto, chango. From Kristy McNichol to Audrey Hepburn in the space of a few short hours." He leaned back in the plush leather executive chair, his long fingers toying with his pen. "I assume I'm to be properly impressed by your maturity and sophistication, or is it another game you're playing?"

She shook her head. "All the games are over now, Steve. I do plead guilty to wanting to look nice for you." She paused deliberately. "For the last time."

Steve muttered a brief but explicit obscenity, his fingers tightening with dangerous force on the pen. "You know damn well you don't mean that."

"I mean every word," Jenny said, her eyes fixed steadily on his frowning face. "I'm not a masochist who enjoys the idea of drawing out a torturous situation. I'm going to opt for a clean break."

"Just like that?" Steve asked, his lips thinning to a hard line. "I suppose this weighty decision was what led you to leave this afternoon. What did you expect to accomplish by that particular bit of insanity?"

"The same thing I'll accomplish when I leave this evening," she said, feeling utterly composed. "The preservation of what's left of my pride and independence. I'm going to do what I meant to do four months ago. I'm going to get a job."

"No!"

"Yes." She paused. "Why did you think I'd changed my mind? The circumstances haven't really altered. I thought for a while they had but you shattered that illusion very quickly. I understand that divorces are very easy to get in Las Vegas. You should be free in no time at all."

He smothered a curse. "You're not getting a divorce!" he said violently.

"I'm afraid I'm not sophisticated enough for one of those civilized separations," she said wryly. "Though I don't doubt you'd find a wife in the background a convenience."

"What do you mean by that?" he asked, frowning.

"Your little playmates wouldn't get any uncomfortable ideas about a more permanent relationship as long as you're married, would they, Steve?"

"I've managed a number of years without that particular type of insurance."

"Then you won't mind being without it now," she said quietly. "As soon as I'm settled, I'll find a lawyer."

"You will not!" The words were shot out like bullets and his eyes were not cool now. They were blazing. "My God, Jenny, I've never seen you so pigheaded. Can't you see that I'm just trying to protect you?"

Her mouth twisted bitterly. "No, I'm afraid I can't see that, Steve. All I can see is a man I foolishly prodded into a commitment he had no intention of making. Don't worry, I'm not about to hold you responsible for what happened last night."

"I didn't say I regretted what happened last night." Steve said thickly. "For God's sake, I thought I'd made it damn clear I enjoyed every minute of it."

"And so did I," Jenny said. "But I find I require a little more from a relationship than you do, Steve. A roll in the hay just isn't enough for me." She drew a deep steadying breath. "I need to know I mean more to you than that. Maybe you were right after all. Perhaps it would have been better if I'd remained your little sister. At least I'd still have something." Her silver eyes were bright with tears. "You may look on me as a child, but I'm adult enough to know when I'm not really wanted."

"Not wanted!" His cool composure blew into atoms. He was suddenly around the desk and pulling her forcefully into his arms. "My God, I'm about to go crazy wanting you," he grated, his mouth covering hers in a kiss of desperate desire. She was stiff with shock for a second before she melted, sliding her arms around his neck and responding to his kiss with all the longing she had stifled. When he raised his head, his eyes were glazed. "Last night wasn't enough," he said raggedly. "I want you all the time." He pressed tiny loving kisses on her arched throat. "I'll never get enough of you."

"I don't understand," she said huskily, her fingers curling in the thick hair at the nape of his neck. "If you feel like that, why won't you let me be everything I want to be to you? Why won't you at least let me try? I may not be all that you want in a woman right now, but I can learn. That's what marriage is all about, isn't it? Learning and growing and building something beautiful together?"

He drew a deep breath and pushed her away from him. "That's what it should be," he said in a hoarse voice. "That's what I want marriage to be for you, Jenny. Can't you see that's why it's so important you don't rush into something that might destroy it for you?" He unwound her arms from around his neck and backed away from her as if she were a high explosive. "The fact that I want you so much it's driving me crazy doesn't really alter anything."

She shook her head, bewildered. "Why?" she asked. "Why are you forcing me to leave you?"

"Don't you know that's the last thing I want you to do?" he snarled like a desperate animal. "Can't you see what you're doing to me?"

"No, I can't see," she said slowly. "But I can tell you what you're doing to me. You're tearing me apart."

"It's nothing to what I'd do to you if I let you have your way," he said hoarsely. "I love you, Jenny. In every possible way that a man can love a woman. You're an obsession that dominates my very existence."

She was motionless. Then a rush of unbelievable joy flooded her. How incredibly, beautifully wonderful! Tears of happiness ran unashamedly down her face. "I love you, too, Steve," she said simply.

He shook his head. "You think you do now."

"I know I do. Now. Tomorrow. Forever."

"You're nineteen, for God's sake," he said, his eyes revealing his torment. "You've had your first taste of sex and you think that's all there is to love."

"I know there's more to it," she said demurely. "I just didn't think you did."

"I know," he said quietly, his face so beautifully tender that it caused her throat to tighten painfully. "I think I've loved you for an eternity. Since the first time I saw you on Santa Flores, I've loved your courage, your endurance, your quiet serenity. You were like a fine jewel shaped by a master, each facet giving off a clear radiance. I'd never wanted anyone to belong to me before, but with you I felt I had a treasure that would be snatched away if I didn't nurture and protect it. I've loved you as a child, as a schoolgirl, and now as a woman. Yes, I know about love, Jenny."

She felt as if golden light flooded every particle of her body. "You certainly had enough feminine diversions," she teased huskily to ease the tension.

"I'm a man," he said, shrugging. "I had to wait a long time for you to grow up." He sighed wearily. "I'm still waiting."

"You don't have to wait any longer," she said, her smile as radiant as a sunrise. "I couldn't love you more than I do now."

"I know you feel something for me; you're too honest not to show it. But how do I know it's not a mixture of gratitude and chemistry? You're much too young to sort out your emotions."

"I wasn't too young for you to take to bed," she said in exasperation.

He flinched. "Yes, you were," he said. "But I was such a bastard that I didn't care."

"I made you angry."

"I used it as an excuse," he said in a tortured voice. "I knew you better than to believe you'd jump into bed with Brody just for the hell of it. But I wanted it to be true, so I'd have a reason to take you to bed myself. I deliberately raped you."

"You didn't rape me," she said indignantly. "*I* seduced you!"

"I admit you nearly drove me crazy with that femme fatale act," he said wryly. "But I'm an experienced man. I'm supposed to have some control."

"But I was so good at it," she said flippantly. "How could you resist me?"

"It was my duty to resist you," he insisted. "I promised myself I'd protect you, not jump into bed with you at the first opportunity."

"It was hardly the first opportunity," Jenny said,

wrinkling her nose impishly. "I gave you plenty of others before you succumbed."

"The fact remains that I'm far too old for you," he said quietly. "Can't you see how much wiser it would be for you to make only a limited commitment to me? In a few years we'll talk about it again. By that time you'll be old enough to make an informed, mature decision."

"No, I can't see that," she said. "I want it *all*, damn it! I don't have any use for this shilly-shallying. I want all of you and I want to give you every bit of me. I want you to admit that we have a future together as well as a past."

Steve drew a shaky breath. "God, you're young," he said wearily, running his hand through his hair. "What the hell am I going to do with you?"

There was annoyed exasperation mixed with a glowing tenderness in her eyes as she recognized the obstinacy on Steve's face. Who would have believed that tough, ruthless Steve Jason would be so idealistically wrong-headed about something that was so important to both of them? How could he be so blind? Couldn't he see this was no teenage infatuation but the love of a lifetime? Her lips tightened in determination. There had been too much waiting and too many misunderstandings already. She wasn't about to permit any more of either if she could help it.

Her gaze ran lovingly over the crisp dark gold hair and the classic beauty of his lean tanned face. "I have a few very definite ideas on that subject, Steve Jason," she said serenely. "You might have had a chance of escaping my toils if you hadn't told me you loved me. But now your goose is well and truly cooked. I'll never give you up now, my love."

"Indeed." Steve's eyes narrowed warily. "And may I ask how you're going to accomplish this coup?"

"Of course. I intend to be quite ruthless in my pursuit of you." She half closed her eyes as she studied him consideringly. "Arguing with you obviously is futile. You're far too bullheaded."

"Bullheaded!" Steve echoed, a trace of indignation in his tone.

Jenny nodded absently. "Persuasion wouldn't work," she decided. "I'll have to use coercion."

Steve's mouth tightened grimly. "What manner of coercion, may I ask?"

She smiled sweetly. "I could tell you that you either give in or I leave tonight and get a job."

"Don't give me ultimatums, Jenny," he said tautly.

She cocked her head and touched one finger to her chin, pretending to ruminate. "Let's see, now. Rex mentioned that his business manager might need some clerical help on his next tour," she lied shamelessly.

"Jenny," Steve warned.

She walked over to him, and her hand toyed idly with the lapel of his jacket. "Don't you think that would be much more interesting than an ordinary office job?" she asked innocently. "Think of all the new places I'd see."

"Jenny, you little devil," he said huskily. "You know I'm not going to let you go on the road with Brody. You're blackmailing me."

"How perceptive of you," Jenny said with a cheerful grin. "That's exactly what I'm doing."

Steve's blue eyes narrowed. "And if I call your bluff?"

"Then I take the job," she said calmly, her gray eyes steady. "And we see who breaks first."

Steve drew a deep breath. "And I thought I was ruthless!"

"Of course, there's always the chance you'll call my bluff and let me leave with Rex," she went on coolly. "In that case I'll just have to get pregnant."

Steve's face paled with white hot fury, his hands tightening on her arms with agonizing force. "I'd kill him!" he said with deadly certainty.

Jenny shook her head at him as if he were a beloved, if slightly addle-witted, child. "Not Rex's baby," she explained patiently. "*Your* baby. I'd really prefer to wait and have a little time alone together, but if that's the only solution, I'll just have to get pregnant."

"My baby?" Steve's voice was dazed and husky. "And how do you expect to conceive this child without my help, my little witch?"

She smiled gently. "But I intend to have your full cooperation, love." She reached up and took one of his strong, brown hands from her shoulder and raised it to her lips to kiss the palm lovingly. "I may be pregnant already, you know."

"What?"

"Well, you're a very virile man, darling, and after

all, I'm half Italian. We're supposed to be very fertile." Her eyes were limpidly wistful. "Would you really want me to go away to some strange city? Pregnant, alone?"

"God, no!" he said hoarsely, closing his eyes in pain at the thought.

She kissed his hand again. "You'll have to keep me with you for a little while to see if I really am pregnant," she said softly. "And I promise you that if I'm not now, I will be by the time the waiting period is over." She smiled up into his face entrancingly. "If you thought I was trying to seduce you before, you haven't seen anything yet. I'll be the most shameless hussy, the most beguiling lover a man could imagine. You'll have to lock me in my room to keep me out of your bed." She slowly lowered his hand and placed it on her abdomen. "Wouldn't you like to feel your baby stirring in me, Steve?" she whispered temptingly, her voice husky with the aching passion that the thought stirred in her loins. She rubbed his hand back and forth so that he could feel the warm, silky flesh beneath the thin material of the cream dress. "Wouldn't you like to put your seed in me, and know that a part of you is growing inside me?"

Steve's chest was heaving with the force of his ragged breathing and his hand moved in helpless compulsion on her belly, as if he could already feel the life within her. His eyes were glazed, his mouth beautifully sensual. "Damn you, Jenny," he whispered brokenly. "Do you know how you're torturing me?"

"I'm a desperate woman," she said softly. "I'm fighting for my life, and I intend to win."

"Oh, God! I think you have." He groaned as he swept her into his arms, holding her breathlessly close as his strong body trembled as it touched hers. "Heaven help you if you don't know what you're doing, because I can't fight you and myself, too. You've had your chance and I'm not letting you go again. It's forever, Jenny."

Jenny's silver eyes shone serenely as she pulled Steve's head down to meet her waiting lips. She said simply, "That's what I've been trying to tell you, love. Forever."